Ghost Dancing

ANNA LINZER

Ghost Dancing

PICADOR USA NEW YORK

Picador® is a U.S. registered trademark and is used by St. Martin's Press under license from Pan Books Limited.

For information on Picador USA Reading Group Guides, as well as ordering, please contact the Trade Marketing department at St. Martin's Press.
Phone: 1-800-221-7945 extension 763
Fax: 212-677-7456
E-mail: trademarketing@stmartins.com

Grateful acknowledgment is made to the following publications in which these stories first appeared:

Kenyon Review, "Ghost Dancing"; *Kenyon Review and Voices of the First Nations,* "The Burial Mound"; *Earth Song, Sky Spirit,* "Sun Offering"; *Raven Chronicles,* "The Indian Rubber Boots"; *Blue Dawn, Red Earth,* "Spirit Curse"; *NW Ethnic News,* "Indian Education."

Design by Pei Loi Koay

Library of Congress Cataloging-in-Publication Data

Linzer, Anna.
    Ghost dancing / Anna Linzer.
        p. cm.
    ISBN 0-312-19548-6 (hc)
    ISBN 0-312-20410-8 (pbk)
    1. Indians of North America—Northwest, Pacific—Fiction. 2. Indians of
North America Oklahoma—Fiction. 3. Family—Northwest, Pacific—Fiction.
4. Family—Oklahoma—Fiction.
    I. Title.
PS3562.I563G48 199
813'.54—dc21
                                                                              98-29648
                                                                              CIP

First Picador USA Paperback Edition: October 1999

10   9   8   7   6   5   4   3   2   1

For Richard, Oscar, Mailani, Eli,
and all our family

Contents

Ghost Dancing

Ghost Dancing

Jimmy One Rock gave the black '62 Impala one last goose and listened to the rhythm of the rattle of the loose fan belt. He flicked off the lights and stepped out. Leaving the door open behind him, he walked to the front of the car, lifted the hood, and shut off the engine. Hank Williams died midsentence.

Jimmy One Rock felt suddenly alone in the dark and silence. The thicket of brush and trees looked an eternity away, across the black open field. He could hear, but not see, the single *pishkw*, nighthawk, swoop as it circled the field in the last pale memory of light in the sky.

One of the last times he'd been out drinking with his brothers, Roy and Chuckie, Chuckie woke up alone in the Impala and thought that the green blinker light on the dash was one of those *manĭtowŭk*, spirits, that Grandma One Rock used to warn them about, and Chuckie tried to climb out the roof, through the dome light. If that light were still there, Jimmy One Rock would have left it on for sure. Even running down the battery would have been okay, just to keep the Impala in sight as he crossed the field. But with no moon tonight, he knew that as soon as he stepped into the field, the Impala, too, would disappear into the night.

Jimmy's feet found the ancient rocky path of his childhood. A cool breath of wind racing down from the stars hit his neck. He pulled up the collar on his black denim jacket and rubbed the worn piece of Grandma One Rock's father's Lenape prayer stick in his pocket. Grandma One Rock had told him that the Milky Way, the ancestor path, crossed this field. When he'd walk it at night with her, she used to sing. Once he asked her about the words she was singing, and she just said, Our blessing, our kinfolks. To fight down the fear he felt in the back of his throat, he sang.

H-e-e-e-e nehani
Latamane
Nehani lamane
Kwenanowagŭn, nowagŭn
Hayelagoma
Gweheyeha
Gehe!

At the end of the open field was a corn garden. Shadows of corn plants and squash vines suddenly sprang out of the flat field and surrounded Jimmy with the summer-night fragrance of wet, watered earth and green plants. Either Roy had decided to plant this year, or Chuckie had found a woman. Maybe Grandma One Rock had come back down that ancestor path and planted that corn.

The last time the corn and squash were planted had been two summers ago, when Lila was still here, married to Chuckie. She had stayed here three corn seasons, leaving finally in the third October. She left Chuckie with the freezer full of elk, the shelves lined with shining Mason and Ball jars packed with green and orange and yellow harvest, the fruit bins full of apples, a tin full of dried shell beans, and all the windows in the house busted out and all the tires on all the cars shot full of holes, even the flat tires of Grandma One Rock's '47 Nash that had the cottonwood coming up through the open trunk.

Their brother Roy moved back in. Roy and Chuckie put a little plastic over the windows, fixed the tires on one of the cars, and ate well for two winters. They joked every time they opened one of those shining Mason or Ball jars that, no shit, Lila was the best wife they'd ever had. They wondered where they'd find one like that for the next winter. And sometimes, after they ate their corn and applesauce and beans, they'd go down to the Red Buck Tavern and look for one.

When Jimmy got to the sagging front porch, he saw that the door was wide open. He found the doorstop jar of matches and lit the kerosene lamp on the wall between Roy and Chuckie's chairs. He had to step through the piles of magazines and western paperbacks on the floor between the two tattered overstuffed chairs.

Jimmy walked across the wooden floor of the small room and saw, in the flickering light of the kerosene lamp, that Grandma One Rock's hide drum was gone. He touched the nail where it had hung and wondered what Chuckie had traded it for. And then the smell of corn chili drew him into the kitchen.

He found the old, soot-covered kitchen lamp in the middle of the table. He lit it, moved away from the sharp smell of burning wick, and stood next to the woodstove at the open kitchen window. Jimmy listened to the songs of frogs coming up from the creek. He ate the lukewarm corn chili out of the blackened pot with the worn wooden spoon and thought about Mary and his sons.

For the past four years, since the Lenape powwows had started up again at Breaker's place just outside of Bartlesville, Oklahoma, he and Mary had packed up the Impala with the boys and dog and presents and drove on down to stay with her cousin, Grace. Every year he meant to stay. And every year, on the second night, just about dark, during the first elders' dances, he'd get this lonely feeling and tell Mary he was going out for a drive and that he'd be back later. Mary probably knew before he did that he was going down to Chuckie's. He had brought Lila and Chuckie back with him the first year, but all three of them got kicked off the powwow grounds for being drunk.

Mary never said anything. Only once, when their oldest son, George, asked if he could go to Chuckie's with him, did Mary ask why he didn't take them all down some year, after the powwow. He didn't answer her, but he could tell by her face that she knew and understood. If he didn't do anything else right, he was at least going to keep his sons from seeing him and Roy and Chuckie drinking again.

Jimmy scraped the last of the corn chili from the pan and put the pan and spoon in the sink and rinsed them with spring water from the jug on the counter. He splashed his face and hands with the cold water, before he blew out the lanterns and stepped out through the rusted, bent screen-door frame.

It was Saturday night. He knew Chuckie and Roy and whoever else happened to show up would be down at the clearing by the creek, next to the stone fireplace left from Old Peter's burned-out cabin.

There were two things that Grandma One Rock, who was actually their great-grandmother, told Jimmy and his brothers about Old Peter. One was that he was a kind of a doctor-man. Friends said that their parents called Old Peter the Devil Doctor, but Grandma One Rock trusted him.

The other thing she told them was that Old Peter should never have built his house down there under that black oak. She wouldn't talk about it, except for one time she said that someone might need to know their names again. When he and his brothers asked her what names, she just answered, *Këlamahpi*. Behave. And then Grandma One Rock gave them

5

that look of hers that meant don't ask any more questions. And they didn't.

Grandma One Rock would never go down to Old Peter's cabin. When she'd visit Lydia Curlyhead, just across the creek and up the hill, she'd go way out of her way to walk around Old Peter's cabin. When Jimmy or his brothers were sick, she'd go out on the back porch and holler down, and Old Peter would always come up. Old Peter was cockeyed, smelled like bear grease, and would dance around their cabin with a mask and prayer sticks, singing and screeching, until Jimmy and his brothers were scared well. It didn't take too many cures until anytime he felt sick, Jimmy One Rock would think about Old Peter and he'd get better. Sometimes when he and his brothers were acting up or wouldn't do their chores, Grandma One Rock would start out toward the back porch, like she was going out to call Old Peter, and they'd straighten up.

One night Old Peter's cabin burned to the ground, with Old Peter in it. It was such a hot fire that, except for the creek-stone chimney, nothing was left, not even Old Peter's bones.

After that, sometimes in the summer, Grandma One Rock would go down alone at night, after Jimmy and his brothers were in bed. The three boys would lie real still and listen to her as she went out the back door, careful not to let the screen door slam, and on down the path. But nobody ever mentioned it in the morning.

Now Jimmy stood outside the kitchen, waiting for his eyes

to adjust to the darkness under the sycamore and for the frogs to start up again. But the night remained silent, so silent that he wondered if he'd ever heard the frogs at all.

That's when he saw the case, just down the path. A whole case of beer, dropped in the path, like some omen. Then he heard it. It was faint at first, as if he were imagining or remembering the sound. But the deeper into the path he went, the more he knew he was hearing the drumming, almost as if he had always expected it, had been waiting, even, to hear it, coming up from the clearing. When he stepped out of the cottonwood grove and saw his brothers Chuckie and Roy and the six Old Ones dancing in a circle around two small fires under the black oak, he wasn't even surprised.

When he was young, Jimmy and his brothers sat by the open fire outside, next to the cabin, and listened to Grandma One Rock's stories, stories of when she had danced, had seen the False Face. She had told them that once—even though she had seen the False Face many times before—at one dance she ran from the Big House, afraid, ran into the woods until her parents followed her and caught her. Even then, she was so afraid that it was decided amongst the elders that to take away her fear she should dance the Spirit Dance and wear the False Face, the Living Solid Face, the *Mĭsinghâlikŭn*. And for some years she did and was the keeper of the mask, the mask that had come across all those miles. It had come for generations along the worn trail the Lenape had been forced to take, away from their tall cedars and clear rivers and blue coastal home waters. It had heard the turtle-shell rattles and the cries of Lenape mourning disease, death, murder, and the unbearable grief of leaving still another graveyard of their ancestors' and their children's bones in exchange for land no one else wanted yet and hollow promises from government agents and missionaries.

Grandma One Rock was the keeper of that False Face until the fear and black despair of the days that followed the end of the Ghost Dance, Sitting Bull's murder, and the massacre at Wounded Knee. Then Grandma One Rock awoke one night with a spirit message in her dream. She got up from her bed on the floor of the cabin and went alone to the creek to bury the False Face under a root of a black oak. The False Face was returned to the spirits.

But there by the two low-burning fires, Jimmy saw that False Face being danced by an Old One, in bearskin pants and shirt, darting in and out, across the fire, through the other dancers. Jimmy recognized the power and felt the fear rise in his veins. But when that Old One, the False Face, shook his turtle-shell rattle and motioned him in, Jimmy took off his shoes and began to circle the fires. And he danced with his brothers and the six Old Ones there, under the black oak tree in Old Peter's yard.

Jimmy could feel the echo of a long distance in the drum. He felt the distance his own song had to travel before the words returned to the fires. And the False Face danced in and out of the circle, up and down, twisting and rising and falling like the yellow flames of the fires. The sound of the turtle-shell rattle and the deer-hide drum and the bare feet hitting the dusty earth became like the beating of Jimmy One Rock's heart. The night passed and was filled with the drum and the song and the dance, until he knew the Old Ones' names and their songs became his blood.

Jimmy's eyes were on the fires, the flames and sparks rising into the darkness, when he felt the first pulling sensation and heard the sucking, like a long breath, come from Old Peter's fireplace. Suddenly fire snakes of flaming sticks and branches rose up from the fires and writhed away along the dust over and up into the stone fireplace. There was a roar up the chimney, and Jimmy felt the pull of every cell in his body. But his feet were locked tight to the earth. As the last fire snake entered the open pit of the fireplace, the roaring became deafening, until it exploded in a huge, crackling fireball above the chimney and into the branches of the black oak. It fractured into a sky of shooting fireball lightning. And just as suddenly came the silence, darkness, and spinning, spinning.

The first sun had just splashed across the edge of the garden when Jimmy awoke and untangled himself from the night. Chuckie's arms and legs and dirty bare feet were all twisted in his own where they lay on the ceiling of the '62 Impala.

Jimmy heard a click, click above his head and looked up to see Roy upside down, still in his seat, turning the key in the ignition.

"What the hell are you doing, Roy?"

"Trying to get this goddamned thing started. But what in the hell are you doing up there upside down?"

"Hell, Roy, you're the one who's upside down."

Jimmy reached up and unbuckled Roy's seat belt. Roy fell with a thud to the ceiling and onto Chuckie.

Chuckie slid out from under Roy and stuck his head out through the leaves at the open window. He whistled a low whistle.

"Hell, Roy, now you've gone and flattened out the whole patch of yellow squash. I knew we should have planted them where Grandma always did, down there on the other side of the beans."

And like his brothers, Jimmy knew, too, that there were some things that couldn't be understood immediately; there were no words for those things. He pulled himself over to the other open window and crawled out.

Standing, he brushed the damp dirt from the elbows of his jacket and slapped his pants legs. Jimmy One Rock looked out at the green sun-splashed field and then leaned back down to his brothers.

"Shit, Roy, you must have been going pretty fast coming off that road. There isn't one goddamned tire track anywhere across this whole goddamned field. Not one. Anywhere."

The Burial Mound

Grandma One Rock's stories had been like mother's milk to Jimmy and Roy and Chuckie. Roy and Chuckie were babies when Grandma One Rock took them in. Jimmy was five then, but his memories of his parents were incomplete, like patches of torn cloth. So to Jimmy it was as if he had been a baby twice, once suckling on a mother he couldn't remember, once on Grandma One Rock's stories.

When Grandma One Rock first told the stories, Jimmy would ask why. Why did the boys get on the turtle's back? Why did they hit the turtle? Why did the turtle go under the water? Was the water cold? Why didn't the boys get off the turtle? Why didn't their grandma dive in and save them? What is an ocean? Couldn't they swim? Why didn't the turtle come up? Where are they now?

11

Grandma One Rock would say, Listen to the story, it will tell you. At first, that would make Jimmy mad. Once after she said that—said Listen—he kicked a pot into the fire and burned his toes. Grandma One Rock never said anything. She wrapped cool mustard leaves on his toes and put him to bed. But the next time she told the story, there were fewer questions, until finally, on the fifth or sixth telling, Jimmy would have no questions. The story would be in his heart, talking to him, telling him what he needed to hear from it.

But Grandma One Rock was gone now. She had died almost five years ago. And now Roy and Chuckie lived in Grandma One Rock's cabin. The first couple of years after she was gone, Chuckie had lived there with Lila. Roy had been living alone in an old trailer in Bartlesville. But after Lila shot the hell out of the tires on Grandma One Rock's old '47 Nash and left, Roy moved back in with Chuckie.

Jimmy and Mary and their sons lived where he could find work, sometimes in Rising Sun, Oklahoma, sometimes on the West Coast with their relations. But every year Jimmy came to Grandma One Rock's place. He couldn't stay away long from his brothers, the land he grew up on, and the memories of Grandma One Rock and her stories.

And so, even now, it was from Grandma One Rock's stories that he knew he must be patient to hear what the spirits of the Old Ones were telling him. Grandma One Rock's stories still spoke to him. And he thought those stories were telling him that understanding didn't always come quickly. But it had seemed like it had gone on forever, that gnawing at his insides, at his heart, that restless feeling. It had felt like a buzzing in his ear that wouldn't go away. At first he thought it was telling him to get drunk. It was like the parched feeling on a hot, still, summer evening when the sun would be low, slanting long across the cornfields, and the thought of a six-pack would start buzzing in his head. The feeling of wanting something so bad it hurt.

It had been three restless days since the June morning when Jimmy and Roy and Chuckie had stepped out of the overturned Impala into the sun. The last few days, watching his brothers tow out his black Impala and replant the squash only intensified that feeling. But Jimmy knew he couldn't speak of it yet. He must listen, listen to what that night was telling him.

Jimmy had let his fingers rub the one small, black, smooth, round rock in his pocket. When he had found it lying in the sun in the middle of the path as he was walking back to the cabin from the belly-up Impala that morning, he knew it was the rock Grandma One Rock had given him years ago when he was a young boy. He hadn't known that he had lost it, or even remembered it, until he saw it there in the dry dirt path.

In all of Jimmy One Rock's life, all the greatest sorrow and all the greatest pride seemed to spring from the same source. Once when he was in bad shape, real bad shape, Mary asked him in her quiet voice what was wrong, and he had said simply, I'm Lenape, goddamn it, a fucking Indian, that's what. His own words echoed in his head for a long time after that, as if to tell him that the only way out of his pit was to climb back up those same words.

Years ago, Grandma One Rock had helped him climb out of that sorrow the first time. On the fifth day he came home from first grade with blood crusted on his face and shirt, Jimmy knew he'd have to talk to Grandma One Rock. But she had been silent. It was a silence that told Jimmy he'd have to ask her for her help. Grandma One Rock was not much bigger than Jimmy was then at age seven, but in her silence sometimes she seemed as strong and ancient and as difficult to ask for help as the giant black oak down by Old Peter's burned-out cabin.

Later that night, after his younger brothers were sleeping next to him, Jimmy got up out of his own blankets on the floor and walked across the cabin to where Grandma One Rock was stirring the last coals in the fire.

Grandma One Rock kept a small tin of tobacco on the mantel next to her red pipestone pipe. On a rare evening she would get down the pipe and tobacco to smoke. Tonight, while Jimmy stood barefoot, shivering, in the fire's light, she prepared the pipe and lit it. In the sweet pungent smoke drifting up to him, Jimmy found the courage to ask Grandma One Rock what he needed to ask her.

"Grandma?"

"Yes."

"I want to change my name."

"Because those boys bloody your nose and call you names."

"They call me Half Boy and One Ball. I don't want my name anymore."

Grandma One Rock puffed on her pipe and stirred the fire. Jimmy sat down on the smooth creek-stone hearth next to her. He pressed against her and felt her warmth through his thin pajamas. She passed the pipe to Jimmy. He held the pipe in his hand for the first time. Grandma One Rock nodded her head, and Jimmy puffed two small puffs. Before he returned the pipe to her, he held it and rubbed the smooth, ancient red stone between his fingers and watched the low light from the fire dance across the red bowl. Grandma One Rock added a piece of thick, gnarled oak branch to the fire.

Grandma One Rock asked Jimmy what name he had chosen. He told her Ivan Johanson. Ivan Johanson rode the school bus with Jimmy. He had slicked-back blond hair and green eyes. He wore real cowboy boots and had his own horse, Silver.

When Jimmy finished speaking, Grandma One Rock puffed on the red pipestone pipe and passed it again to Jimmy. Then she told him that one day Jimmy's father, Henry One Rock, had been beaten up and thrown in the freezing winter creek by five boys in his class. An older girl had helped him out and told him to say his name was French. She told Henry that her uncle was French, too, and she understood. So by the time he got home, he had decided to call himself Billy French.

Grandma One Rock laughed and said, "Billy French, Billy French."

With one small, dark hand, Grandma One Rock flipped the burning oak branch and added two dry apple branches. The flames rose and lit up her face. Jimmy watched the lines around her mouth, waiting for her to speak again. Sometimes he thought he could see a story form on her face, around her mouth, in her eyes. He was always looking for a story there, trying to read her eyes, like the corn planter reads the sky for signs of rain.

"This is the way it was told to me. My Grandfather One Rock, he was just a boy. He was walking alone in the cornfield. The *pisim,* the corn, was very high. On the far end of the field a man stood as tall as the corn. He tossed an *ashëna,* a rock, to One Rock. It was a small, round, white rock. One Rock caught it and swallowed it and looked back up.

" '*Kwik! Kwik! Kwik!* The ducks have a praying meeting in the fall of the year!' The man was really a *kwikwingëm,* a duck. Half black, half white.

"One Rock knew what he must do. This duck spirit had told him. He kept the ceremony in the fall for that duck spirit, for all *kwikwingëm.*

"He told his people of his blessing. He would pound his chest and bring back up to his hand that *ashëna,* that one rock given by his duck spirit.

"Lawulĕnjei wŭjegŭk toxweyu.
Kwĕnanowagŭ wailagomaole Lĕnape.

16

Eli nanŭ telowa.
Lowa nuni, ĕndageko lowaet, lowa nŭni.

When he opened his hand something came out of the center.
That's his blessing for our kinfolks, the Lenape.
Because that is what he said.
He did say this, when he spoke, he said this."

Grandma One Rock put her hand in Jimmy's. When he looked down, he saw a small, round, black rock in his open hand.

"That is for you. You listen to that rock. It will tell you your name."

Grandma One Rock put away the pipe and the tobacco tin. Before she went to her quilt in the corner, next to the wooden clothes chest, she touched the top of Jimmy's head. Jimmy sat alone on the hearth, looking at the round, black rock. Even when he climbed under his blankets, the flickering embers of the fire tossed out enough light into the cabin for him to see the shining black rock in his open hand.

"Hell, Jimmy, we don't need no fucking sweat lodge. You just wait another month, and it'll be so hot here, you'll be sweating all you want, and then some."

Roy lifted an armful of kindling from the pile around his feet and threw it into a large, dented tin bucket. "Here, you load this in the bin by the woodstove and bring it back. We've got to get this kindling in. If we don't, old Ida Coffeepot will just help herself. She's got some kind of kindling detector on me. Every time I chop a mess of this juniper kindling, she shows up with one excuse or another for a visit and some hard-luck story, and I end up giving her half my pile."

Jimmy cradled the full bucket in his arms, sucking in the fresh, sharp smell of the eastern red cedar sticks. "This sweat lodge is what the spirits of those Old Ones were telling me I need to do."

Roy put his hatchet down, lifted his Redskins cap, and smoothed back his straight black hair. He turned to Jimmy. "Hell, you know what they were telling me?"

"What?" Jimmy set the kindling bucket back down to listen.

"Well, that night those spirits were telling me, clear as if it had been Chuckie speaking, 'Before this night is over, Roy-man, you're going to need to replant your whole goddamned patch of yellow squash.'" Roy laughed and picked up his hatchet again and started splitting, speaking over the crack of the metal opening the grain of the red, dry wood. "Hell, Jimmy, if it'll keep those spirits from flipping your Impala onto the squash plants, I'm all for a sweat lodge."

"I'm thinking of building it in the cottonwoods on the far side of the creek, across that little plank bridge going to Lydia Curlyhead's place. That bridge still there?"

Roy got real quiet and turned to stare out through the sycamores in the direction of the plank bridge, as if he could see it from there. "I was across it while the sun was coming up this morning. I found an eagle feather for you. I hung it on a low branch above where I found it, about where I thought you'd want that lodge of yours."

Jimmy and Roy stood together gazing out toward the stream, lost in their thoughts and memories just long enough for Ida Coffeepot to see them there, clear as day, in the bright morning sun.

After Roy used some of the juniper kindling to start a fire in the cookstove and fry up some eggs and sausage and hominy grits, Chuckie and Jimmy headed out to work on the Impala, behind the woodshed where they'd towed it. Roy set out with Ida Coffeepot, in the blue truck, loaded with a big pile of his kindling. He was going to drop her and her load of fresh-split kindling off at her place on the way to Big Al's Junkyard to get a radiator and a fan belt for the Impala.

Jimmy and Chuckie worked together to pound up the flattened roof of the Impala and wire the hinges on the hood. There wasn't any real rush. Mary wouldn't expect Jimmy to show up until the weekend. So Chuckie and Jimmy took their time and stopped their pounding often to lean across the seats or over the hood to talk.

"Chuckie, you ever been in a sweat?"

"No, Jimmy, I can't say that I have. Old Peter had some sort of sweat house down by his place. You remember it?"

"No."

"Roy and I used to climb up on the roof of the woodshed in

the winter when all the leaves were down and spy on Old
Peter," said Chuckie. "You must have been in school by then,
I guess. Anyway, we'd used these telescopes we made out of old
rolled-up dog-food sacks. We thought we could see Old Peter
better with them, sort of zoom in on him. A couple of times we
saw him down by a little hut, toward the creek from his cabin.
One minute he'd be hunched over a little low-burning fire next
to the hut, the next minute he'd just disappear. Later on, he'd
reappear, naked and as red as the sun, and run on down to the
creek and jump in. Once there was even snow on the ground,
and he rolled around on the big snowbank first. Well, the way
the hut was so low down, sort of into the ground, we figured
Old Peter had himself a tunnel under there, dug clear down to
Hell. And that's why he was so red and hot when he came up.
Scared us pretty bad, maybe that's why we didn't tell you. Or
else we thought you'd tell Grandma on us and we'd catch it
then, for spying on Old Peter." Chuckie laughed. "You ever
been in a sweat, Jimmy?"

"Never have. But I met a Cheyenne once, when I was in
prison. He told me about his sweat at his grandfather's house."

"Shit, Jimmy, you never told us you were in prison."

"It wasn't long. Just a few months. Long enough to dry
me out."

"What were you in for?"

"A sandwich, I guess. I'd walked into the Little Teepee Tavern. Heard they had good buffalo steak sandwiches. But I met
Art Arthur, the owner. Remember him?"

"Not that I'd want to."

"I guess I punched him out when he took me back to the front door and showed me the sign on the door that said 'No Shirts, No Shoes, No Service, No Indians,' and asked me if I could read. The judge told me I held up my left hand to Art Arthur's face and asked him if he could read that, and then I sucker punched him with my right. Flattened him. I don't remember it, I'd just come from Art Arthur's Heap Good Tavern across the street. It had a sign on it that said 'Indians Welcome.' I could read that."

Jimmy was glad to tell Chuckie that story and laugh with him. It had been a particularly dark time for Jimmy, that whole year when he was drinking so bad. The worst part, though, was that Mary took the baby and went to her aunt and uncle's place in Bartlesville to wait for Jimmy to quit drinking.

What Jimmy remembered most often about that year alone was which bush and stump and fence post and rusting car body had hidden one of the many bottles of fortified wine he'd stored along the four-mile road into Rising Sun to make the walk tolerable. Finally, though, the high school kids in the cars that drove up and down and up and down that road caught on, and he couldn't keep a bottle hidden from them long enough to unscrew the lid. And then, trying to get a sandwich, he ended up in prison instead. Mary had come back with the baby when he got out, and his life began again.

"I'm going to build a sweat lodge tomorrow, Chuckie. Down in the cottonwoods, by the plank bridge Grandma used to get over to Lydia's. We'll have a sweat on Friday, before I have to get back to Mary. I thought if we got this here Impala put back together, I'd drive into town and find Albert Curlyhead. I thought I should talk to an elder, to get some sacred advice for the sweat."

"Well, just drive on by Albert Curlyhead's, then. I heard that last week he was up at the Pentecostal church preaching against the Stomp Dance and against wearing feathers and beads and devil symbols. Shit, Jimmy, if I were you, I wouldn't advertise what I was doing. It's not just a sandwich at the Little Teepee. A sweat lodge might get you a trip to an Oklahoma prison, too. And I'm not just shitting you. A powwow is one thing. A sweat lodge, that's something else."

Chuckie pulled out a black-and-white bandanna from his hip pocket and wiped his forehead. He squinted up at the sky. His gold front tooth flashed in the midday sun. "It's getting hot out here, I think we should go get some of Roy's coffee. He left us a Thermos on the table. We'll just quit this for a while and wait for Roy."

In the pale evening light coming through the dark shadows of the waxy cottonwood leaves, Jimmy could almost see the sweat lodge as he had imagined it, not the patched, dirty, black plastic lean-to that it was. But Jimmy knew that not everything is revealed at once. He tried to remember that, as he held Grandma One Rock's red stone pipe, a pipe that had never before, in Grandma One Rock's hands, failed to light, but refused to light now.

Jimmy set the pipe next to the low, hot fire, and sprinkled tobacco around glowing creek rocks and on the path of the doorway to the lodge. He uttered bits and pieces of prayer he remembered from Grandma One Rock.

"*Nuxa. Kishelëmieng. Tëmakelëminen. Wëli nipalinèn. Winëweokan. Gata lapèmkwësi.* Father. Creator! Take pity on us. Stand us up well. Pleading. I want to be useful."

The details of the sweat had not been revealed to Jimmy One Rock in the spirit visit, and Roy and Chuckie helped him flesh it out, gathering the plastic, bringing dry split wood, and using the asbestos gloves to move the burning red rocks into the sweat.

Jimmy knew there were moments that could only be called sacred after enough days had passed to remove any memory of anxiety, pain, and doubt. But at the instant the flap of plastic was opened and they each entered the dark, musty, hot interior, Jimmy felt it was a sacred time. Nothing else existed.

It was many pure, full minutes before anyone spoke. The heat and steam and darkness began to penetrate their skin. In this dark, quiet womb it was natural that Grandma One Rock came to their hearts first. She was the only mother they had known. She had held them in their growing as firmly and as surely as the earth they sat on. Her old Lenape ways set her apart and yet joined them to their history and people, filled with mystery, deep enough for a lifetime. The brothers were bound together in this mystery.

"*Gëtëmaktunhe.* I talk humbly. Grandma One Rock told us to listen. Remember, sometimes, even at night in the quiet and darkness she'd say, *Këlamahpi,* behave, listen, there is a story in everything." Jimmy could feel the sharp burning in his lungs from the steam as he spoke.

There was a long quiet before Chuckie spoke. "I hear Grandma One Rock's Nash telling us it doesn't want to get rusty out there with the cottonwood growing out of its trunk."

Jimmy wanted to say, Shit, Chuckie, this is a sweat, not a goddamned garage. But he kept quiet and listened to Chuckie.

"That eagle feather, Jimmy's black rock, the red stone pipe," Chuckie continued. "They're telling us to care for the bones of our ancestors. That car sits out there in the weather like the skull of a dead elder uncle. The other cars don't bother me none. But that one, ever since Lila shot the tires off, it's been trying to tell us something."

Grandma One Rock drove the Nash only a few times before Jimmy was big enough to take over most of the driving for her. The first time she drove it was when her niece's cousin came from the West Coast and brought her a station wagon full of sweet grass. Grandma One Rock sat alone on the little porch with the Nash parked right in front. She scraped and slimed the mucus from some of the sweet-grass blades, until finally

Grandma One Rock stood up and walked to the shed. She dragged out the two big pieces of plywood Uncle Jake had given her to patch the woodshed. She laid a small bundle of sweet grass between the sheets of plywood, right there in front of the Nash. She got in the Nash and started up that shiny brown and white car and drove up onto the plywood. All the rest of that afternoon she jerked the car back and forth, back and forth, across the plywood, her forehead barely visible in the window, squeezing the mucus right out of the sweet grass.

Grandma One Rock made many fine baskets that summer and sold them all to a woman who drove all the way from Albuquerque to buy them. Grandma One Rock told her she had used an ancient method, passed down from her ancestors, to clean the sweet-grass stems. When Uncle Jake heard that, he teased her, but Grandma One Rock said her ancestors taught her to use well what was given to her, and then she laughed.

The second time she drove the car was to the new drive-in theater. That year the raffle tickets from the Indian Days Parade and Pancake Breakfast were being drawn at the Big Moose Drive-In. Grandma One Rock never missed a drawing. But Uncle Jake, who usually drove them in, was gone for the weekend, so she loaded the boys into the Nash and drove all the way to the Big Moose in first gear. At intermission, the drawing was held and Chuckie won the new blue Schwinn bike with training wheels.

After the movie was over, Chuckie got on his new bike.

Grandma One Rock turned on the high beams in the Nash, and in the light of the headlights of Grandma's '47 Nash, Chuckie rode his new blue bike with training wheels all the way home.

Jimmy and Roy stuck their heads out the open windows into the warm summer air and shouted encouragement to Chuckie. The training wheels were worn down to the metal by the time he pulled up to the cabin. Roy unbolted them the next morning. Roy and Jimmy later stripped the bike and sold it to their cousin, Luther Curlyhead, for seventy-five cents.

In the heat of the sweat, their memories and the silence that extended into the darkness were broken suddenly by the simultaneous crash of thunder and flash of lightning. Every pinhole and rip in the plastic was lit up, momentarily cutting open that fragile darkness.

The sacred pure moment of the sweat's beginning was now lost in its flailing, painfully lingering collapse. The wind-torn, mud-splattered plastic flapped around the three brothers as they dressed next to the steaming, sputtering embers. Jimmy tucked the wet eagle feather into his T-shirt next to his skin. Rain was already running down his neck, clear to his belt.

Out of the wind and rain came the sound of a horn honking above them, from near the cabin. Voices called down to them.

Jimmy stayed behind, alone in his humility and confusion, wondering if he'd heard the Old Ones wrong, if he hadn't been listening after all. And if he had, why was he standing there wet, half-naked in the middle of the night, feeling empty and lost? He rubbed the smooth, black rock between his fingers and tried to listen to the night storm as it crashed around him and soaked him.

When Jimmy stooped to pick up Grandma One Rock's wet, red stone pipe, illuminated in another, now more distant flash of lightning, he heard the high-pitched laughter of women and Roy and Chuckie's deeper voices, and he heard the doors slam and a loud, fast car drive away into the night. Jimmy felt utterly alone.

In the quietest, darkest hours of the night, after the rainstorm passed and the moon set, before the June sun rose, Jimmy sat alone on the sagging porch of the old cabin. As the sun came up over the cornfield and down the path to the leaves of the sycamore, he watched the mist rise like a sweet sigh from the green earth and understood in his bones what had called him into the sweat lodge and what had cast him out. It was all of the same breath, the same sighing, breathing earth. Water, fire. Darkness, light. Breath from his lungs, breath from his ancestors.

Wetёndẹis, One Who Is Like Fire, the scarlet tanager, sang out as if it were trying to fill the morning air, until its coarse song joined even the sound of the rain-swollen creek, running full and swift below the cabin. But the cabin was quiet and dark. Jimmy was alone in the sunrise.

Without Roy in the kitchen to light the fire, make the coffee, and fry the eggs and ham and hominy, breakfast was cold and meager. But Jimmy's fast before the sweat had left him with a huge hunger. Sitting back on the porch steps with a can of cold beans and a mug of leftover coffee gave him time to imagine digging a hole big enough for Grandma One Rock's '47 Nash.

When he walked out onto the field and stood next to the old brown Nash, rusty shovel in one hand, a water jug in the other, and the sun already hot on his back, Jimmy had to laugh out loud. At least Grandma One Rock had managed to get the smoking, coughing Nash as far as the edge of the garden, where the soil was fine and deep and easy to dig. It had been the Nash's last trip to Ida Coffeepot's, and Grandma One Rock's last, too. She had died the next day. But not without first giving Chuckie the coveted red-and-white-speckled bean seeds Ida Coffeepot had finally shared with her. She told Chuckie she was going to be gone at bean-planting time and that he needed to plant the beans for her. He didn't understand her words until later. But he planted her beans that spring and every spring since. Even when the rest of the garden seemed to go to hell, Chuckie always tended those beans.

The sun rose high in the clear Oklahoma sky, and Jimmy's steady digging continued, until he was deep into a large hole. The empty water jug sat on the ground next to his sweaty black T-shirt. The rust was worn off the shovel, and the handle was polished smooth and shiny from his callused hands and sweat. He only heard Chuckie and Roy arrive just as they pulled up in the '52 Chev pickup and the doors opened and slammed shut.

Chuckie called out, "Shit, Jimmy. I think you've been away from the reservation too long. What, you forget how to live on Indian time?"

"Hell, Chuckie. Maybe he's got himself one of those ancestor rocks."

"Shoot, yeah. Fill this hole in with a load of chicken shit, and the whole fucking reservation'll be fixed for tomatoes."

When Jimmy and Roy and Chuckie were young, one of their spring jobs, early in the morning and in the late evening, while Grandma One Rock weeded and hoed and planted, was to gather the rocks she turned up in the garden. They would fill a bucket and haul it to the road and dump it out. The long dirt road across the field, leading out to the main road to town, was still firm with the rocks hauled in during the hundreds of barefoot trips across the field. And rock by rock, bucket by bucket, the road had been built.

On nights when the twisted road across the field shone in the moonlight, Grandma One Rock would say, See how it shines like the stars. The ancestors have come down their Ancestor Path, the Milky Way, walking this road at night, blessing it, leaving little bits of those stars behind.

And that would scare Jimmy and his brothers half to death, thinking of ghosts walking their road while they were sleeping. After Grandma One Rock told them about the ancestors coming down that path, whenever they had to go out at night, they always made just a little noise, quietly clapping their hands or singing softly, to let those ghost spirits know they were coming. They figured ghosts and snakes were a lot alike, and it was best not to come upon them by surprise.

Grandma One Rock had them pile the biggest rocks, rocks that were too big to put on the road, up behind the house. She gave them no explanation. Just, *Këlamahpi*. Behave. Do what I say. Then one summer Albert Curlyhead came and dug out a well at the little spring and built a stone wellhouse with all those big rocks. All but one. That one still stands high next to the wellhouse.

One Sunday morning Chuckie complained that one of the rocks was too big to dig up. Grandma One Rock would not hear of it. *Këlamahpi*. Behave. Do what I say. Jimmy and Roy and Chuckie dug all day while Grandma One Rock was across the stream trading seeds and gossip with Lydia Curlyhead and Ida Coffeepot.

But late that night, after Grandma One Rock smoked her pipe on the porch and came in to sleep on her quilt on the floor, Chuckie woke Jimmy and Roy. The three brothers went out the kitchen, around the cabin, and back to the garden.

In the light of the full moon, making just enough noise to warn the spirits, Jimmy started up the Nash. And while Roy stood on the seat next to him, to give him directions, Jimmy drove out to the big rock at the edge of the garden.

The moon was down low in the rustling cottonwoods when Chuckie and Roy and Jimmy, dirty and tired, crawled back into their blankets. All the chains and cables and ropes and

Grandma One Rock's '47 Nash were back in place. But that big rock was next to the pile of rocks behind the cabin.

The sun was already high when Grandma One Rock woke them to a big breakfast of black coffee and cornmeal mush and ham and sugared fry bread and a bowl of wild strawberries.

All through their meal she stood over them and said, *Mitsikw,* You eat!

As soon as the last sweet berry was eaten she said, *Kòchëming atàm,* Let's go outside. They followed her silently out the kitchen door and to the rock pile, where she said, See, in the night the ancestors threw down a piece of that Ancestor Path. And she took them to the giant hole. They stood at its edge while Grandma One Rock told them how that rock had bounced there and rolled along the deep, newly cut trail to where it stood. The brothers silently listened. Then Grandma One Rock went alone into the kitchen. When she returned, she gave them a big hunk of dried elk meat, fresh biscuits wrapped in brown paper, and a Mason jar full of hot coffee tied all in a towel and told them, This is a day to remember, the day the ancestor rock came down. No school today. And Chuckie and Roy and Jimmy all shouted, *Sipung atàm,* Let's go to the creek. They ran down the path before Grandma One Rock could discover their trick and send them down the road to school.

Grandma One Rock spent the day alone in the garden mixing buckets of chicken manure with soil and filling in the giant hole. There were never sweeter or redder or bigger tomatoes in

Grandma One Rock's garden as the ones that grew that year in that spot. Each time they ate a tomato from those plants, Grandma One Rock would say, You thank your ancestors for those tomatoes. And over the years the story grew and changed and became as present on that land as that giant boulder of a rock next to the wellhouse.

By the time Jimmy wiped the sweat from his face with his dirty red kerchief and climbed up out of the hole, Chuckie was already hooking up the cables to the Nash. Jimmy stepped into the shade of the cab of '52 Chev truck and took the fresh jug of water Roy handed him. He started to raise the jug to his mouth, then stopped and set it down on the running board. He watched Lila cross the far end of the garden and walk up on the porch and disappear into the cabin.

Jimmy turned to Roy. "That was Lila that came in last night?"

"Yeah. Came in from Anadarko with some nieces of Ida Coffeepot. Think she's planning on staying awhile."

"Cabin'll be a little smaller with three of you now."

"Yeah, been thinking the same thing."

"Mary and the boys are always glad to see you. I'll be leaving in a day or two. You might want to come along."

"Might do that," said Roy. "Just might do that."

Jimmy drank the water from the jug, tossed it back onto the floor of the cab, and he and Roy joined Chuckie at the back of the truck where Chuckie pulled more cable and chain and pulleys from the rough, wooden, oil-stained Buckskin Bullseye Shot box.

And the three brothers began to move together steadily and deliberately in the unforgiving heat of the Oklahoma sun. They worked together with few words at their ancient, practiced art. It was a dance, really. And the music of the dance entered their breath, the flex of their muscles, the lift of their shoulders, the beat of their pulse, the sweat of their backs, and the weight and pull of the chains in their hands. When the cables were secure and tight, and Chuckie was at the wheel, Roy gave the motion to go forward. Jimmy watched the final, slow-motion arch and leap and fall of Grandma One Rock's '47 Nash as it rose and then settled into the cool earthen grave.

The brothers spoke little as they filled in the hole, shovel by shovel full. Sweaty and hungry and spent from their labor, they returned to the cabin and ate hot chili and corn.

Afterwards, Jimmy lay on a blanket under the sycamore. He fell asleep to the sounds of Chuckie's voice and Lila's laughter, the scrape of pans, the slosh of water, and the clink of glasses and dishes. The sound mingled in his sleep until a dream of Mary woke him with a longing, an aching close to sadness. He stood and returned to his shovel, knowing he'd leave in the morning. Knowing that as the sun was coming up, he'd already be on his way to get Mary and the boys in Bartlesville, and that they'd all be on the coast, at Uncle's, before the week was out.

It was later in the evening, as the sun was slanting low across the cornfield, when the brothers tamped the last of the earth onto the mound that held Grandma One Rock's '47 Nash. The shadows of the sycamore and the cottonwoods were stretching and dancing in the breeze out in the field where the three men stood.

They each leaned on a shovel, their backs to the house and the setting sun, their eyes on the smooth dark mound, a mound caused by Jimmy's miscalculation of a few shovels of dirt. When the brothers had filled dirt in the hole around the Nash, the brown, rounded dome stuck up out of the field like the top of a giant rotting skull.

"Hell, for all we know, Jimmy," said Chuckie, "this was meant to be. Yessir, for all we know, this might just be the continuation of some ancient Lenape burial mound culture."

"Yeah," said Roy. "And in about five days, Chuckie, you're bound to wake up to some anthropologist and his half-clothed female assistants all sniffing around here, asking questions. But I'm afraid you're going to have to handle this one alone. 'Cause now that Lila's back to see that you don't starve out here, I think I'll head out with Jimmy for a while."

"I expect I'll just leave all those anthropologists to Lila. She never was one to tolerate people sniffing around here. The half-naked female type, especially." Chuckie laid down his shovel, took off his cap, and ran his fingers through his thick, curly hair. Keeping his eyes on the mound, he said, "But you two, you're always welcome here. This place is yours, too. Always will be." He put his Redskins cap back on, setting the bill down close over his eyes. "Well, I guess there is just one thing left before you two leave."

Roy and Jimmy stood by the mound and watched as Chuckie walked across the field and into the shadows near the cabin. Chuckie was the shortest of the brothers, but always the strongest. Grandma One Rock used to tell him he had one of those canoe bodies. He was built for a canoe: short legs, small hips, broad, powerful shoulders and arms. Ah, what is a Lenape canoe-body doing out in Oklahoma, I'd like to know, Grandma One Rock used to say. Sometimes she would laugh, too, and add, Oh, but that tide's going to rise up from the east. The Lenape will smell that salt air again, you boys just wait and see. A wave! * Òngùndëwakàn!* A blessing. And then she'd laugh, imagining. Grandma One Rock had never once seen the salt water, but the memory lived in her bones; the tide still pulled at the blood beating in her veins.

Sometimes, when they were young and there wasn't anything else to do, Jimmy and Roy and Chuckie used to climb up on the roof of the wellhouse and cup their hands over their eyes and look out to the east, out over the garden and the cornfield and the road, and wait for that long, salty wave to roll in across Arkansas.

When Chuckie returned to Jimmy and Roy, he held up a thick stick of coiled grapevine, three stems twisted tight around each other. Snakevines, Grandma One Rock used to say.

Chuckie walked up on the center of the mound and stuck the end of it into the earth. Without speaking, Jimmy and Roy followed Chuckie.

Jimmy touched the smooth wood of the twisted grapevine and remembered the same feel on his fingers of Grandma One Rock's twelve prayer sticks. He pulled out his red and black kerchief from his pocket and tore it into twelve strips. As he tied each strip to the end of the stick, he called out a prayer, Ho-o-o. And with each prayer, his voice rose higher, as if to reach and join some ancient spirit voices coming from the earth, the sky, dancing with the ghosts of memory in his bones, forever calling out those twelve ancient prayers.

Roy took his leather tobacco pouch from his back pocket, unwrapped the thin leather thongs, and spilled tobacco on the earth around the coiled stick for a blessing, an offering. Jimmy pulled the red stone pipe from his vest pocket. It lit easily. As they stood silently together under the darkening sky, Jimmy shared the pipe with his brothers.

Chuckie reached out and touched the coiled stick and said, "This stick is to remember this day, to remember our Grandma One Rock who drove this Nash, to remember that we are brothers, and to remember that we belong to this place." He laughed quietly. "Maybe, someday, when we're old, Jimmy's grandsons can read about the Oklahoma Lenape Burial Mound in some schoolbook and tell us what it means, these . . ."

"Symbols."

"Yeah. Symbols."

Jimmy put his hands on Roy's and Chuckie's shoulders, and the three brothers headed back across the field. They walked toward the light of the kerosene lamp burning low in the window, hungry for the food Lila would be cooking for them, each imagining what they loved most.

The Hunt

"Hell, Roy, since you put in new springs and shocks, we're riding so smooth, this old dirt road feels like it's been steam pressed." Jimmy One Rock switched on the round, black radio knob and waited for it to warm up. The windows were rolled down, the Oklahoma sky was a never-ending blue, and Jimmy and his brother Roy were heading east, right into the rising sun.

Roy patted the leatherette dashboard. "Maybe she just knows you and Mary will be taking her home, and that by next week she'll be sleeping under the cool green branches of a giant cedar tree instead of tits-up in some dusty cornfield."

Hank Williams was singing "I'm in the Jailhouse Now" on the radio. Jimmy turned it up and tapped his fingers on the padded steering wheel. His eyes moved over the flat land around him. The bumpy road ran along Lone Cherokee Creek, where sycamores, oaks, and cottonwood grew lush and tall and green. Beyond the creek, small cornfields, dry grass, and bare, rocky earth stretched flat and far into the day.

"Sometimes, when I drive along here, I think of buffalo," said Jimmy. "Like I can hear the sounds of their running on the earth, hear that snorting bellow they make, taste the dust in the wind."

"Hell, Jimmy. When have you ever even seen a buffalo?"

"I don't know. Must have been those cowboy movies Grandma One Rock used to take us to on dollar night at the Big Moose Drive-In. But still, I think about buffalo along here."

Roy adjusted the visor on his Redskins cap, pulling it down low over his eyes, and squinted out into the blast of yellow sunlight. "I used to love it when Grandma One Rock told us stories of that big buffalo swamp up north. And all those sacred, all-nations hunting grounds."

"Shit, yeah. I'd almost forgotten those stories. It was her Uncle Rains Hard that told her those stories, wasn't it? He was the one who lived to be over a hundred, like Grandma One Rock, wasn't he?"

"Between the two of them, they go way back, those stories."

"Wasn't until I was in Miss Whitener's class in sixth grade that I realized those places weren't still there, that she'd been talking about places in Pennsylvania and Kentucky that were long lost."

"No fences, no paper laws. I liked to hear her tell those stories."

"Hell, I hardly see a deer along here now."

"Chuckie and I have been going way up past Deaf Lake to find anything big enough to shoot."

"Too much is gone. No buffalo. Streams drying up. Sometimes I wonder what's happening. Oil wells, highways, stinking factories, fences everywhere."

"Shit, Jimmy, seems like anytime I'm driving along in some little town, looking around, thinking like that, out comes a state patrolman and I get pulled over. And he'll say, 'Hey, Indian, what in the hell do you think you're doing here? Get your red ass out of this country before I lock you up.' And I wonder, does he know something I don't know? But maybe they just left our chapter out of the history books in those big, fine universities they go to." Roy reached into his pocket and pulled out his pack of Camels and lit two cigarettes and passed one to Jimmy. "Shit, yeah, it's like they think Columbus landed, knocked on the door, and said, 'Anybody home?' and the Three Little Indians said, 'Oh, come on in, make yourself at home. Pocahontas will show you around. We were just getting ready to walk to Oklahoma.' "

"With no food. Barefoot."

Jimmy and Roy laughed and then sped on in silence, smoking and watching for hawks circling the fields, ravens and crows picking at dusty, drying roadkill, magpies flitting through the tall grass, and meadowlarks calling from their fence perches. For many miles they were alone in their thoughts, with only Hank Williams and Patsy Cline to remind them of sad times.

Jimmy first spotted the white '65 Belair station wagon way off in the distance. It was gleaming in the sun like some glowing meteorite, stopped in the middle of the narrow road, doors thrown open, children and dogs everywhere.

"Hell, must be some bad accident. Shit. By the time an ambulance gets here, they'll just have to scrape the fried bodies off the road with a spatula."

"Some kind of accident, Jimmy. Looks like there's just one car. Must be car trouble. I'll get my tools out of the back."

Jimmy eased the Impala to the edge of the road. He left the engine running. But even so, he could hear the clear water sound of the creek below as it ran and spread out into a small, muddy swamp. The steady call of blackbirds rang up from the cattails. A warm wind was coming off the field across the road. Jimmy pulled his Cleveland Indians cap down securely on his head and tucked in the flapping tail of his denim work shirt.

Walking out to the center line and toward the car, Jimmy first heard the hiss of the radiator, then saw the extended legs, the splash of blood in the dust, the crown of antlers. It took Jimmy a moment to understand the sudden tense, panicked look of the man. Roy sensed it first and hesitated at the open trunk of the Impala.

The man motioned his wife and children and dogs back toward the car. Jimmy glanced back at Roy for only a second, seeing that he, too, noticed the New York license plates and the bumper stickers: UNITED PRESBYTERIANS FOR INTEGRATION, CHRISTIAN CHILDREN'S FUND, SEE AMERICA WITH GREEN STAMPS.

The woman gasped and said, "Gordy, they're Indians!"

Gordy motioned his wife to keep quiet. "Lock the doors, Jane, keep the kids down. I'll take care of this."

A blur of children and dogs was followed by doors slamming and locks snapping shut. Then there was perfect silence, broken only by the rustle of the wind in the cottonwood and the one repeating song of a red-winged blackbird.

Jimmy reached in his back pocket. Gordy's hands shot straight up in the air like two jet-powered white rockets. A sob rose from deep within the car. Jimmy pulled out his wallet, flipped it open to his BIA card. He flashed it in the sun and said, "Officer Six Killer, Sioux Warrior Society Tribal Game Warden." Jimmy slid his wallet back into his pocket and circled Gordy, keeping his eyes on the buck.

"I see you've killed a buck."

Gordy now had his hands dangling uncomfortably at his sides. But when he spoke, they shot out again in nervous gestures. "I didn't see it. It must have come up from the creek."

"This is not buck season."

"Sir. I didn't mean to." Gordy's voice cracked. "I didn't mean to."

"It's a federal offense to poach deer on the reservation."

"Oh, sir, I didn't mean to. I didn't mean to."

Roy stood back in stony silence, watching the scene, admiring Jimmy, drinking in the fresh Oklahoma June morning, the rising heat, the promise of the day.

"I see you are from out of state."

"Yes, sir. We're just passing through. We'll be out of here as soon as we can. Just as soon as we can."

"Officer Longknife," Jimmy said to Roy, "I could use some help here."

"Sir, is there a fine I can pay?" Gordy reached into his pocket and pulled out his own thick wallet. "I can pay the fine."

Jimmy paused, looked at the buck, saw a bubble of bloody foam rise from the deer's nostril, saw the twitch of its leg, took his hat off, ran his hand through his short black hair and looked back at Gordy.

"Well, ordinarily it's a prison sentence."

"Oh my God, oh my God."

Jimmy gently nudged the buck. In one last death spasm the deer rose on its front legs, arching its head and full antlers into the air. Gordy jumped straight back. In the car, Jane started screaming and crying uncontrollably. Then the children started crying, and the three dogs were barking and lunging and drooling up against the windows.

Roy pulled his buck knife from his pocket, approached the twitching deer and swiftly, skillfully, slit its throat. The rush of blood puddled and ran in crooked streams through the dust and rocks on the road.

Roy looked up at Gordy. Sweat was running down Gordy's

face. Roy felt pity as he watched the man turn a horrible shade of gray. Then Roy turned back to the buck, saying a silent prayer. Roy wiped his knife on his jeans, folded it shut, and put it back in his pocket.

Jimmy spoke to Gordy again. "Well, sir, you are from out of town. Is this your first offense?"

"Oh yes, sir."

"Well. We want you to enjoy yourself here in Indian Country. So if you'll donate the venison from this buck to the Kikewinu Boys Home, I guess we can overlook it this time."

"Oh yes, sir. I mean yes, I'll donate it, yes, I will. Yes sir. Thank you, sir. Yes. We are enjoying ourselves. My wife and I have always been interested in Indians. Yes, sir."

After Gordy helped Roy and Jimmy load the six-point buck into the trunk of the Impala, he thanked Roy and Jimmy over and over, shook their hands, and had his wife and children roll down the windows and meet the Sioux Warrior Officers.

Gordy shook their hands once more and gave Jimmy four crisp one-hundred-dollar bills for the Kikewinu Boys Home.

As Jimmy and Roy got into the Impala, Jimmy raised his hand and called out, *"Welakwshia."* Gordy nodded his head solemnly.

Roy whispered, *"Welakwshia?"*

"Old Lenape word. Sacred word," said Jimmy. "Means intestine."

Jimmy and Roy fell into the car in a fit of laughter and roared out into the road, passing the smiling, thankful faces in the freshly dented white Belair station wagon, knowing that with the busted radiator, Gordy and Jane had a long, hot day ahead of them in Indian Country.

Jimmy held up the four crisp one-hundred-dollar bills. They fluttered and rustled in the hot wind coming in the windows. "This Sioux Warrior hereby donates this money to the *Kikewinu* Boys Home. The Middle-Aged Boys Home."

"Good thing Grandma One Rock didn't hear you call yourself a Sioux."

"He's from New York. Hell, he's living on the land of our Old Ones. The bones of our ancestors are under his steel buildings. Why would he worry about a couple of stray Lenape? And besides, they've got such short memories up there, if I'd of said Lenape, he'd of thought I was a French chef."

They drove on down the road until Jimmy found the turnoff to Lost Arrow Lake. They pulled into one of their old drinking spots under the cottonwoods and gutted and skinned and butchered the buck. They wrapped the small hunks of meat in cool cattail leaves.

All the rest of the afternoon, as the sun rose and passed over and behind the black '62 Impala, they sped on down the dusty road. They imagined again and again Mary's pride when they would present the fresh venison to her relations. A gift to the elders from the hunt.

Wild Indian Dogs

When they saw the cars lining the dirt driveway, parked up on the weedy, dusty lawn, Jimmy and Roy knew why they had been thinking of Uncle Arnie all day. Hardly an hour passed that day, beginning at sunrise when they were docking the boat at Neah Bay, that one of them wasn't remembering some story about Uncle Arnie. Most of the stories were funny, and they kept laughing clear until just before sunset, when they stopped to get some water from the creek along the old Johnson Road. But they grew quiet when a black cloud of crows tumbled out of a gnarled maple tree at the far edge of the field. A single white crow turned and circled back around the wide field, calling out to them, before it disappeared in the dark line of trees across the creek.

When Jimmy parked the Impala up on the grass behind a

black truck, he knew, and though neither of them spoke, he knew Roy knew, too. Out of the car, they stood and stretched, letting the solid click of their doors shut out the long dusty miles, the roar of the engine, the sound of the radio. In the sweet, still September night air, they each adjusted their eyes and ears and hearts to where they were.

The lingering warm fall had stirred the frogs, and over the sound of their croaking, Jimmy could hear children laughing and calling in the yard along the creek that fed into the small swamp above the beach. For a moment he was lost in a memory of sounds that hurled him back to Oklahoma, to the field next to Grandma One Rock's garden where he and his brothers and cousins had played in the night air of their childhood. But the memory was broken by the squeak of the rusty hinges on the trunk as Roy opened it. Jimmy focused back into the darkness and on his brother.

"Here, give me some of those." Jimmy held out his arms for Roy to fill with fresh salmon, wrapped in damp newspaper, cool from the plastic sacks of ice packed around them.

"Too quiet for a party," Roy said.

"Hell, yeah. I was thinking the same thing."

"And the kids are still out."

Both Jimmy and Roy knew that if it was anyone but an elder, the children wouldn't be playing outside. But sometimes when an elder passed on, it seemed natural for the kids to keep playing.

Jimmy and Roy had taken Uncle Arnie's Neah Bay boat out alone for the first time this summer. Uncle Arnie had had surgery in the spring and figured he'd need one summer to get his strength back and that maybe, if the run was good, he'd do a little gillnetting in the sound in the fall.

Fishing hadn't been good so far this year, and Jimmy and Roy had had to go farther north than they had hoped. And with Mary caring for Uncle Arnie and working in the cannery, Jimmy and Mary hadn't seen each other for over two months.

It wasn't easy for Jimmy to walk up the path now toward the light of Uncle Arnie's house, feeling pulled by thoughts of Mary, pushed by sadness and loss. He watched the door to the house open briefly, and through the lower branches of the ancient cedar, Jimmy could see three figures step out onto the porch, silhouetted against the lighted window.

"Hey, who goes there?" a voice called from the porch.

"Hey, man. Roy and Jimmy here. That you? Cousin George?"

"Roy and Jimmy. Hell, we was just talking about you. Mary's been leaving messages between here and Neah Bay since he passed on this evening. How the fuck you get here so fast?"

"Uncle Arnie, huh. When did he go?"

"Just a couple of hours ago. About sunset. Here, have a beer. Cigarette?" George said. "Hey, what you got there?"

"Fresh king," Jimmy said. "Get that refrigerator door, will you, Cousin George?" George was Mary's second cousin, but Jimmy, like most everyone else, called him Cousin George.

There were so many Georges on the reservation that each George had an identifying title. Jimmy's own son was a George. But the name, the title, fit Cousin George so well that Jimmy thought that even if he were the only George on the rez he'd still be Cousin George.

George helped them carry the salmon onto the porch, and he and the Flo-Lows, the twins Floyd and Lloyd, stacked them on the bottom shelf of the old porch refrigerator. Everyone, even their grandmother, called Floyd and Lloyd Flo-Low or the Flo-Lows. Once Jimmy overheard a visitor ask which was which. Their grandmother just answered, Floyd, Lloyd, Flo-Low, all the same.

"Fishing's not so good, I hear," said Flo-Low.

"Hell, Flo-Low. Jimmy don't want to talk fish, get the fuck away from the door," George said. "Let him through to his woman."

Flo-Low stumbled and lurched toward the railing. Jimmy opened the rusty, torn screen door and turned the dented, black door handle and took a deep breath. Then he stepped into the kitchen and into the swirl of cigarette smoke, curling and circling up to the bare bulb above the women sitting together at the red Formica table.

"Jimmy. Oh, God," Aunt Lucy sobbed and rose from her chair. "I didn't think you'd get here before they took him." Jimmy held Lucy's small, plump body in his arms, feeling her tremble against him. Lucy was Uncle Arnie's wife, making her

Jimmy's relation by marriage. But she was also Mary's blood relation. Aunt Lucy and Uncle Arnie's marriage was a strong one,
tying two tribes, two histories, and joining many people as rel-
atives.

"Where is he, Auntie?"

"He's in the bedroom." Aunt Lucy pulled back. "You go on
in there."

Jimmy's eyes took in the room, recognizing the faces of Lucy
and Arnie's friends and relations. He could hear the low hum
of talking in the front room.

"Auntie, you come back in with me, will you?"

Jimmy held Aunt Lucy's cool, small hand in his. As he
turned to walk toward the bedroom of his ancient uncle, Mary
came into the kitchen. Jimmy reached for Mary. His fingers lin-
gered a moment in her straight black hair, then slid onto the
warm, smooth curve of her neck. He pulled her to his side.

The bedroom was darkened. A small lamp was hanging on
the wall to the side of Uncle Arnie's iron bed. The shade, like
the walls, was smoke-stained brown and let out only a small circle of light, reflected again and again in each of the wavy, night-
blackened panes of the window. And in the center of the circle
of light, in the center of the room, lay Uncle Arnie.

Uncle Arnie was wearing a clean white long-john shirt. His
brown bony hands were folded across his chest just on the
edge of the yellow cotton blanket that covered his thin body
and legs. His head was thrown back and his mouth was open,

as if there were some final word, some final thought, to explain this, to leave them with.

Aunt Lucy cried softly. Mary moaned and rocked against Jimmy. Jimmy felt his own chest tighten and the tears well in his eyes. To see the body of his once powerful uncle so small, so old, broke his heart.

"I told him good-bye today," Mary whispered. "He knew. He was so clear and peaceful today. He knew. He told me good-bye...." Mary's voice broke, and Aunt Lucy's voice filled in the silence.

"It was right after you left that he took worse. Been about a month. We all knew it was coming. This last week he couldn't even eat, the cancer was so bad. He knew. He said the Old Ones visited him. They were here with him. He said that. Sometimes they'd be singing or drumming." Aunt Lucy stopped to catch her breath. "One day, last week, in the evening, he said, 'They're here. They are with me now.' And I asked him, 'Are they drumming?' And he says, 'No.' So I says, 'Singing?' And he says, 'No.' And I said, real quiet, 'What are they doing, Arnie?' And he says, 'Playing poker.' "

Mary and Jimmy quietly laughed.

"But this week he's been talking about a girl, a young girl, telling him to follow her, all flirty with him, teasing him, calling him to her, and then she'd turn and say, 'No, you can't come with me now.' Of course, I wanted to be sure it wasn't somebody I knew. Or he knew." Aunt Lucy laughed softly and then wiped away a tear. "And she's been here most of the week. Was sitting in that chair one day." Aunt Lucy pointed to the straight-back chair in the corner. "Yesterday I caught a look at her, from the corner of my eye, just for a moment. She was all soft and brown, wearing one of those old cedar dresses." She paused and caught her breath again. "Today she must have come again. And this time she let him follow."

Jimmy reached across the bed and touched Uncle Arnie's hand. Arnie's skin was so soft, so loose from the bone, that Jimmy was almost not sure he had touched him. He bent down and cradled Uncle Arnie's head in his arms, resting his cheek against his uncle's forehead.

"Thanks," whispered Jimmy. "Thanks, old man, for all the good times. I'm going to miss you."

Aunt Lucy cried softly and quietly walked out of the bedroom and into the kitchen. Lucy's crying was muffled by the thin walls that separated the two rooms. Jimmy held on to Mary and patted Uncle Arnie's arm.

Standing at the bedside with Mary, Jimmy knew two gifts. One was the gift of Grandma One Rock, who, like a small brown stone that had been tossed from her eastern ancestral lands, had stayed firm on the Oklahoma land. The other gift was from Grandma One Rock's brother, Frank Moses, who was blown with the wind and pulled by the tide to a shore his ancestors knew only in dreams. Jimmy knew he had been joined, by both gifts, to Mary. And he knew that those gifts had passed down to their four sons, each with Grandma One Rock's prairie grass singing in his heart and the two oceans of ancient uncles beating in his veins.

Jimmy reached into his jacket pocket, pulled out his worn leather tobacco pouch, and pinched out some tobacco, first for Mary and then for himself. They each sprinkled the tobacco around Uncle Arnie.

"Good journey, Uncle."

"We'll be coming along one of these days, too."

"*Nĕmuxu̱mës, mushha̱kòt. Ikalia̱,*" Jimmy spoke the language of the Lenape. "Great-uncle, the sky is so clear. Go."

"*haʔɫ kʷ(i) adsəslabcəbut,*" Mary spoke the language of the Salish. "Watch over yourself well, Uncle."

Jimmy put his arm gently around Mary's shoulder. "Let's go sit with Aunt Lucy now. Then I want to go find those boys of mine."

But as they stepped from the bedside, they turned to see Reverend Falfer and Marvin in the doorway. Reverend Falfer was the pastor of the local church. Marvin was his constant companion. Most people just called him Reverend Falfer's altar boy and left it at that. Falfer had a reputation of a criminal past that was longer than the long black cloak he always wore. He claimed Jesus had reformed him, but there were jokes about his using white powder and whiskey in his sacraments. As Aunt Lucy said, she might turn the other cheek, but she wouldn't dare shut even one eye when Reverend Falfer was in her house.

Jimmy was startled by the new addition of Reverend Falfer's high, bright red Mohawk, a scruffy crow-and-seagull-feather fan held in his hand, a long string of bright glass beads dangling from the handle. Marvin was wearing a shining, wrinkled, cheap suit.

"Oh, Uncle. We have come to help you on your journey to the Happy Hunting Grounds," said Reverend Falfer.

Reverend Falfer held the fan high as he stepped into the room and next to the bed, opposite Mary and Jimmy. Marvin took his place at the foot of the bed.

Reverend Falfer instructed Marvin to light the sage. He began to chant slowly, his outstretched arms keeping time, stopping only twice to try to close Uncle's mouth. He spoke in a high chanting voice, "My brother and I have come to lead you on to the Happy Hunting Grounds as my people have always done. My people know what you need for your trip. We are here to help you."

As Reverend Falfer began to chant again, Jimmy realized he recognized the chant, but couldn't remember where he had heard it. He listened and watched until he realized it was the same beat as the song on the cartoon the boys watched on TV, "Powwow the Indian Boy."

"My brothers and sisters," Reverend Falfer said. "Lift with me. Lift the bed, turn it so Grandfather's head will be to the west, so Grandfather's soul can travel west to the land of his people, the people of the setting sun." Reverend Falfer and

Marvin each stood at one of the bed's corners and motioned to Jimmy and Mary to join them. Reverend Falfer continued chanting to the tune of "Powwow the Indian Boy."

Jimmy felt Mary tense. She broke from his side and put both of her hands squarely down on the bed. Aunt Lucy, who was now standing in the shadows, stepped in the doorway and said softly, "Mary, what religion is this?"

Reverend Falfer answered, "The religion of your people. The ancient religion of our people. My people have taught me."

Mary leaned toward Aunt Lucy, put her hand out to her, and said, "Auntie, go to the kitchen and start a fresh pot of coffee. Good and strong. Wait for us in the kitchen, Auntie."

Jimmy stood behind Mary. Jimmy did not understand what Mary was doing, but he trusted what he heard in her voice.

"There are some things we need for this ceremony," said Mary. "Some of Uncle's sacred things."

"Yes, sacred medicine will help him on his way."

Mary reached above Uncle Arnie to the cluttered top of his chest of drawers and picked up an eagle feather with a beaded staff and three long ribbons.

Reverend Falfer stood tall and nodded his head as he reached for the eagle feather. But Mary held it tight in her hand above Uncle's head.

"I will hold Uncle's eagle feather," she said. "But you must reach in Uncle's closet behind you and get his little Stihl chain saw."

"Chain saw?" Reverend Falfer's voice cracked.

"It was gifted to Uncle in the giveaway at Makah this spring. It is important for this ceremony," said Mary.

Reverend Falfer motioned to Marvin, and Marvin rummaged around in the tiny closet until he pulled out the gleaming chain saw.

Mary looked at Marvin and nodded solemnly and said, "Now you must start it and give it to Reverend Falfer."

"This is a sacred ceremony. An Indian ceremony." Reverend Falfer's head bobbed as he spoke, and his red Mohawk cast long shadows, first on one side of his head and then on the other. "I don't need a chain saw to conduct this sacred ceremony."

"Well." Mary spoke slowly and carefully. "To do that sacred ceremony, to help Uncle's spirit find its way, you are going to need to start up that chain saw and use it."

"Use it?"

"You are going to cut Uncle in half."

Jimmy heard Reverend Falfer's and Marvin's breaths draw in, and then they were deathly quiet, waiting for Mary to speak again.

"You must understand, Uncle's half Lenape, from the land where the sun rises. So I guess half of him needs to face the east, you know."

Reverend Falfer was stopped still. A little pile of embers, falling from Marvin's burning sage, glowed on the blanket at Uncle Arnie's feet. Mary reached out and flicked them to the floor.

"And," continued Mary, "if you don't understand this part of the ceremony, maybe you should go out behind the house. I'm sure one of my cousins could teach it to you. But they're traditionals. They use a broken beer bottle."

Mary laid the eagle feather gently across Uncle Arnie's chest. Jimmy followed Reverend Falfer and Marvin out through the kitchen. Chairs scooted aside, and the door swung open for them to leave as Mary joined her aunts for steaming hot coffee sweetened with sugar and thick, fresh cream.

Jimmy stood on the porch in the half circle of light coming out through the kitchen window and watched Reverend Falfer and Marvin disappear into the night. Flo-Low handed him a cigarette. Jimmy picked up a beer from the case next to the stairs. He opened it with the church key tied to the dirty string that Uncle Arnie kept nailed to the porch post, and then set the opened beer on the wide rail.

"Well, looks like old Falfer's gone native, huh," said Roy.

"Shit," said Flo-Low. "Yeah. A couple of nights ago he was over at our place, about three sheets to the wind. I wasn't in too great shape myself. So Falfer, he asks me for a haircut. And I say, 'You want my Indian special,' and he says, 'Hell, yes.' That's when I gave him that Mohawk. Funny thing, I saw him the next day, and he says he likes it and starts carrying on about some damn drop of Indian blood."

"Well, looks like that drop hit flood tide tonight."

"Shit, yeah."

"Hell, from looking at him and Marvin, I'd say one of them had a Cherokee princess for a grandfather."

They all laughed, opened more beers, and grew quiet. A soft breeze had come up, and the night suddenly smelled of fermenting ripe blackberries and cool salty kelp and seaweed.

And as he listened into the night, Jimmy understood that what he had witnessed in Uncle's room, he had seen many times before. Drunks becoming Indian experts, sniffing around death like dogs at the smell of blood. Christian priests trying to win souls, befriend The Indian at the graveside.

Once, when he and his brothers were young in Oklahoma, they were with Grandma One Rock at the funeral of one of her friends. The priest went on and on about how The Priest was The Friend of The Indian, The Church was The Friend of The Indian, The Indian was always welcome in The Church. It was hot, and Jimmy and Roy and Chuckie were uncomfortable in their tight, stiff clothes. And Chuckie whispered, Who the hell is The Indian, being so damn friendly, always getting us stuck in these fucking pews. I'd like to beat the crap out of him. Jimmy and Roy and Chuckie got snickering so loud that Grandma One Rock smacked them each on the head with her fan.

So Jimmy knew. He knew that death brought them all out, ready to brag and promise and lead the way. Sniffing around like dogs.

Jimmy's mind drifted off into the night as he listened to hear the dull, steady pounding of the waves on the beach below. A lone heron, disturbed, screamed out as it flew through the trees, finally settling in a branch in another tall fir nearer the house. From up on the hill there came an echoing howl of dogs.

"Pack of dogs, huh," said Jimmy.

"Yeah. It seems like no matter what," said George, "there are always four or five dogs living out in the woods. Always have been. But all of a sudden, it's got the folks up in town all worked up. I laugh every time I read the newspaper. Every week there are articles, warnings about baby-eating rabid dogs. Letters, shit like that. You'd think there were hundreds, that we were down here breeding monster dogs. Talked to that cop that lives down from the station. Said they're hiring him for a special investigation. Way he sees it, he'll get paid to walk up the streams and do a little trout fishing. Looking for those wild dogs. Wild Indian dogs."

Cousin George took a drink of beer before he continued. "Shit. I think half of them this year must be mine. The way it is, you go fishing or to the woods for a month or two, throw some bones in the yard as you leave, call out to the Flo-Lows to feed the dog. Sometimes they do. Sometimes they don't. Sometimes the old dog'll be there when you get back, sometimes it won't."

"Kind of like your woman, huh, Cousin George," said Roy.

George laughed. "Hell, I guess that's the way it is."

. . .

The howls and yips grew and echoed. Jimmy stared out into the dark. The dogs gave a depth to the night, a spirit to the woods, a voice to his own fears. But his thoughts were broken by the sound of metal hitting dirt, by the searching flashes of headlights through the trees, twisting down the long dirt road.

"Whoever it is, is sure riding low. Polishing his belly tonight," said Jimmy.

"Must be old Ralph," said Flo-Low. "He's so cheap he'll be pushing that crate of a hearse in a red wagon before he fixes the front end. Last time he was at the station, I told him he needed new ball joints, but no, 'Just change the oil and put in gas,' he says. Good thing he just hauls dead bodies around, 'cause I sure in hell wouldn't get in that death trap alive."

"Maybe that's why he drove over the graves in the cemetery at Soozie's burial last month. Saving gas by not driving around the back way," said George.

"What? He drove over the graves?"

"Yep. He had his flunky driving. And there's old Ralph, standing right in the middle of the graveyard, directing that flunky to just roll that hearse right in over all those grave markers."

"I would have liked to have grabbed him right then and smashed his face in," said Flo-Low.

"Well, then right in the middle of Aunt Lucy's song, he says, real loud, 'Move on in, there's plenty of room up here.' I had to hold Aunt Lucy back then, or she'd have killed him," said George.

"Shit," said Jimmy. "Why in the hell is he coming for Uncle, then?"

"Hell, Jimmy," said Flo-Low. "There's nobody else that'll come out to this part of the rez. In town maybe, but not down here."

The door to the house opened. Aunt Lucy came out in a shaft of smoky light streaming from the kitchen. She had a black cardigan sweater thrown over her shoulders, but still she shivered in the warm night air. Jimmy put his arm around her.

"Is that him?" she said softly. "Is that that undertaker?"

"We'll be right here. We'll stay with Uncle as they carry him out, Auntie," said Jimmy.

Mary stepped out behind Lucy and whispered, "We're here, Auntie."

"Yes. But I don't want to be here when he leaves, when they carry him out."

"I'll walk with you next door. All the kids went over there. We'll go see them," said Mary. "Jimmy'll stay here and be sure they're gentle with Uncle."

Mary led Aunt Lucy down the stairs and along the narrow path through the garden to the house next door just as the hearse rounded the last bend in the road and flooded the yard with its light. The doors opened, and Ralph and his assistant tumbled out.

"Hey," Ralph called out. "We in the right place? Is this the Moses place?"

"This is Arnie Moses's house," Flo-Low answered.

"That's one hell of a driveway. But I thought I recognized the place. This is the same Moses place where we picked up the bodies of those two little girls that drowned a while back, isn't it?"

Jimmy could hear the breath draw in and sense the muscles tighten. George muttered something and spit off the porch. But no one answered Ralph. Ralph and his assistant unloaded and carried the narrow stretcher up the stairs and started to go on in the open door. Jimmy put his foot out against the stretcher leg.

"Maybe you should see if the family is ready for you first."

"Well, I got a call to come. And nobody likes to keep a dead body around. I get in as fast as I can. That's what folks want." Ralph pushed the stretcher to one side and stamped his black shoes on the doorjamb, loosening some old dirt clods.

"You ready in here?" he called in loudly as he entered the kitchen. Ralph and his assistant walked over toward the bedroom door and called in, "You done in there? Another ten minutes be okay?"

And at that, Roy and Jimmy flew in one perfect motion across the kitchen and into the tight entryway leading into the bedroom, pinning Ralph and his assistant up against the wall, smashing their noses flat into the wallboard.

Jimmy spoke quietly into Ralph's ear. "Now, Mr. Under-taker. We are going to go back out on that porch again. And you are going to walk down those stairs and get in that big fucking hearse of yours and wait for us to bring Arnie to you. You understand?"

"Yes. Yes, I do," said Ralph into the wall.

As Jimmy and Roy each quietly escorted one of the men back through the kitchen, Aunt Lucy's sisters silently nodded in approval. Back in the kitchen, Aunt Lucy's oldest sister motioned them to the sink to wash up before they handled Uncle.

After Uncle was gently lifted into the hearse, Jimmy and Roy returned to the porch and said good night to the aunts and cousins and relations as they walked and rode away into the night. Doors slammed, tires squealed, voices called out. And then Jimmy and Roy were alone in the night on the porch.

Jimmy could hear Mary gathering their boys on the porch next door, and he listened to them call back to their cousins as they started down to the little cabin on the beach. In his mind, he could see Mary walking in a pale stream of moonlight, he could see the motion of her hips, her slender bare feet on the soft, sandy earth. He ached to touch her, to feel her skin against his, to be sure of his own presence on this earth.

Aunt Lucy came up out of the shadows under the cedar. She stopped at the stairs and looked up at Jimmy and Roy.

"Roy, you can stay here tonight. I've got that good sofa bed in the front room. And Jimmy, you go on down to Mary now; I'll be okay. I'll be okay."

Aunt Lucy paused and said, "But Jimmy, I've got to warn you." And then she paused again and pulled out a pack of cigarettes from her sweater pocket. She tamped one out and lit it with her shaky fingers. "I've got to tell you, be careful. There's a pack of wild dogs out tonight. A whole pack of them, I'd say. And some of them's been sniffing around this place tonight."

Then Aunt Lucy laughed softly. And Jimmy and Roy watched Aunt Lucy as she walked up the stairs, through the kitchen, and into the bedroom to be alone. From behind them, up on the hill, came one long, low howl. And Jimmy and Roy understood. They knew just what Aunt Lucy meant.

Sun Offering

Jimmy rolled over, opened his eyes, and squinted into the brilliant September sunlight flooding through the window onto the bed. A freighter had crossed the bay. Huge breakers were hitting the shore below the cabin, crashing against the pebbles and drift logs.

He stood up and stretched and went out the small door next to the bed to stand in the tall wet grass to watch the last of the waves. With each crash, he could feel the pounding vibration in the cool earth under his bare feet. The waves passed as quickly as they came, leaving only the long echo as they raced down the curve of the beach toward the long sandy spit at the end of the bay. Jimmy was lost for a minute in the sweet breathing rhythm of the tide rising and falling against the pebbles.

Jimmy had come to know that every place has its rhythms,

its own music. When he had first come from his home in Oklahoma to this bay, he found that rhythm in water: the waves, the tides, the flooding streams, the soft rain in the leaves, and the hard rain pelting the rusty tin roof of Uncle's cabin.

And coming now from two months of fishing in the Pacific, Jimmy felt the softness of the rhythms in this bay, the sounds of water muffled by the shelter of all the lush green. This place, this bay, was as different from the harsh unprotected beat of water and wind and blinding sun out on the ocean as it was from the land of his home in Oklahoma. Jimmy drew in a deep breath of cool salt air and felt a shiver run down his spine.

Listening past the sound of the waves, Jimmy heard the muffled crowing of the little red bantam rooster and the quieter pleading cries of his five barred rock hens coming from the locked interior of the '52 Chev wagon where they safely spent their nights. Jimmy knew he had time to slip on his jeans and meet Mary across the field. In the five days since Uncle had died, Jimmy had not touched Mary. From respect. From fear.

Every morning since he'd been back from fishing, Mary got up with the sun and the banty rooster. She grabbed Jimmy's old red plaid wool shirt off the nail by the door and covered her shoulders and thin white cotton nightgown and slipped out the door.

Most mornings, Jimmy would lie in bed and listen to her pick up the water cans, and half asleep, he'd imagine her as she walked down the path through the tall stubble grasses and thistles across the weedy yard into the cedars. From there, she would follow the cool, dark path of deer fern, maidenhair fern, and vanilla leaf at the small stream flooding out into the bay just below the cabin. And there, standing barefoot on the smooth, flat stone at the edge of the deepest pool, she'd bend down and fill the water can.

Buttoning his jeans, Jimmy went back in the open door. He moved quietly, hoping not to waken their sleeping sons. Slipping on his T-shirt, he listened again for the banty rooster, but heard instead a low, scraping sound.

Jimmy froze, his blood running suddenly cold. Even in the light of morning, Jimmy was wary. How to explain this feeling, this fear, but in days? The days counting from death.

Uncle's death, like midday sun on glass shards, lit the fragments of Uncle's cultures. Memories of ghost walkers, of lodges burned, water left, food baskets filled, songs sung, vigils kept, games played, stories told, all to set those ghosts, those spirits, free. Death became the sunlight on the shards of Uncle's two ancestries: East Coast Lenape people thrown across mountains and land to Oklahoma, and West Coast Salish people, scattered along the beach by disease and lies and allotments. Each flashed memories and stories, filling Jimmy with fear and aching, both for what he knew and for what he did not know. Ghosts of the recently dead with ghosts of memory and of stories he knew and stories he would never know had been dancing around the cabin.

Aunt Lucy had felt it too. She had seen the light dancing across the bright shards and had begun to remember what she had not thought she'd ever known. At first, she'd cried and wanted to burn the cabin, remembering her grandmother's stories of the dead. Even a Christian burial could not stop the fear for Uncle's wandering spirit, for her own safety from other long-forgotten spirits. And Jimmy and Roy remembered Grandma One Rock's stories. Aunt Lucy remembered her great-grandmother's stories. Finally, Jimmy and Roy and George and the Flo-Lows went to Lucy's house. They took down the door and door frame that Uncle's body had been carried out through and burned it, turning their faces from the flames, and replaced it with a door and frame from the old shed. And a calm came back to Lucy. She sprinkled cedar around the door. She cooked salmon and clams on the beach, and family gathered around the fire and ate and told stories and laughed late into the night. Feeling safe then, Jimmy and Aunt Lucy joked about whether Uncle's spirit would take the long Lenape path of twelve days or the short Salish path of three days.

But the scrape, scrape made Jimmy know that Grandma One Rock, Uncle's father's sister, told the truth in her stories of twelve days, twelve traveling days for the Lenape spirit to get to the other side. He tried to joke with himself that maybe the west was a little closer to that spirit place, since they needed only three. Or maybe the Lenape just took their time. But Jimmy couldn't help himself for counting back, checking the number of days since Uncle had died. The scrape, scrape pierced through him.

Jimmy had seen too much in his life to leave his sons alone in the cabin with that sound of scratching on the earth coming up to them from under the floor. Some of the old stories told of spirits that looked for young, strong companions to join them on their final journey. Jimmy could never really believe that. But still, he'd seen too much in his life.

Jimmy put his head against the door to hear their sweet muffled breathing. Even in his fear he hated to wake them. Opening the door a crack, he saw them together, curled in a warm slumber ball of pillows and blankets and young, fresh, sweet brown skin on the horsehair mattress on the floor in the corner.

No matter where the boys were, how far apart in the cabin they were when they fell asleep, they seemed to roll like marbles on the slanted floor into that corner. The Inseparables, Jimmy called them. Roy shortened it to the Rebels. And seeing them there, their young, strong bodies in the darkened corner, Jimmy thought of Grandma One Rock and of Uncle Arnie and of how they each had been so shrunken, so small, so old when they died, as if they each had been dried brown puffballs, blowing the life of the next generations out in their last breaths. And here, in this cabin, they grew, these sons of his.

The scratching was broken by a clink, like rock to rock, or metal on rock. George, Jimmy's oldest son, heard the sound too, and sat up. He jumped up and, not seeing Jimmy, ran to the sound, and before Jimmy could speak or follow, the three youngest tumbled out and across the room behind the cookstove and under the sink.

Following his sons, Jimmy came around the corner into the kitchen in time to see four small butts in the air and a longer body sprawled out on the kitchen floor. All the heads seemed to be pulled down under the sink as if they were being eaten by the scrape, scraping sound, which was louder now. Jimmy walked toward the sink and hunched down, almost kicking over a tin can half full of long, wriggling worms.

"What the hell . . ." Jimmy said. "What the hell's going on?"

Muffled voices came up from under the sink, echoing in the leaky pipes.

"Worms, Papa."

"Big. Big worms."

"Joey's getting worms."

"Joey's going fishing, Papa," said George's voice. "This is Joey's best place for worms. Joey said we could get worms here. And he's taking us fishing this morning."

Jimmy remembered the story Mary had told him the night after Uncle died, as they lay whispering in bed, waiting for the boys to fall asleep. While Jimmy had been gone fishing for the last two months, things had happened that Mary was only beginning to tell him.

Joey's dad's being in jail was one. For drinking water, is how Mary said it. Sometimes when he felt lazy, instead of getting water at the creek, Louie used to drive to the vacant cabin at the top of the hill. The owners lived in Seattle and camped at the cabin only two or three times each summer. Between the visits, they hired Louie to mow the grass and keep the blackberry vines from taking over. They left the water on in the summer and had Louie shut it off and drain the pipes for the winter. On the days Louie worked there or checked the place, he would fill his water cans from the hose.

This particular morning, Mary told Jimmy, Louie had gone to get water at the cabin and found the place pretty well trashed, doors busted in, windows broken, furniture on the lawn. He filled his water cans, and as he went to leave, picked up one of the broken chairs to take home and nail and glue back together for Angie. Louie was handy that way. That night, the sheriff came to his house and found the chair, accusing Louie of wrecking the cabin and stealing furniture. But in court, the real proof seemed to be the Rainier beer can the sheriff found in Louie's truck. It seems that the cabin was littered with beer cans, one short of a case. All Rainier. And, as the expert witness testified, Indians drink Rainier beer. Lots of Rainier beer.

The minute Angie heard Louie had five years to serve, she took off with his cousin Henry, leaving Joey alone. After the trial, Joey cried and wailed and wouldn't go home with any of his relations. That night, Aunt Lucy walked down to Louie's cabin and found Joey and asked him if he was any good at catching fish. He said he was pretty good. So she told him to catch her a good mess of fish in the morning and bring them to her; she'd have the fire in the woodstove going good and hot and the skillet greased. The sun was barely up when Joey got to her house in the morning, and he'd been staying there ever since, fishing for her most every day. He'd get barnacles or mussels or little crabs or worms for bait, depending on where he was fishing, what he was fishing for. Mary just hadn't bothered to tell Jimmy where Joey got his worms.

Another handful of moist, black dirt mixed with slender chips of rotted wood landed at Jimmy's feet. Three worms were plunked into the waiting can, followed by satisfied sighs of approval. Jimmy patted the four backsides, and then leaned down and gently squeezed one of Joey's ankles.

"Catch a couple extra. I'm pretty hungry. You bring Aunt Lucy down here, and we'll fry us up a mess of those fish when you get back," Jimmy called over his shoulder. "Because I'm not eating no worms for breakfast."

The banty rooster took up crowing again. Even without looking toward the '52 Chev wagon, Jimmy knew that the tap, tap he heard was the banty rooster pecking frantically at the rolled-up windows. But Jimmy didn't look in the direction of the rooster in the Chev. He kept his eyes on Mary.

Mary's black hair was loose and long down her shoulders. The red plaid shirt was open and Jimmy watched her as she walked toward the old Buick, across the grass from the Chev, and he saw the fullness and motion of her breasts and hips under her thin cotton gown like a vision from some dream. Jimmy felt the heat of desire rise as warm in his blood as the heat of the sun on his skin.

Mary saw Jimmy then. She set down the water cans and waved at him, and then she turned and ran up along the edge of the grass to the Buick. Jimmy followed her and watched her open the trunk. He saw the curve of her dark legs and thighs as her gown lifted as she leaned down into the trunk.

Uncle Arnie's '47 Buick had long been engineless and windowless, a hiding place for boys, a nest for squirrels and mice and swallows. But it still had the tightest trunk on the reservation, perfect for keeping the chickens' corn dry and the mice out.

Mary stood next to the Buick, each of her arms extended, holding coffee cans brimming with sweet yellow corn high in her hands, like some perfect sun offering. Jimmy came up behind Mary. He reached around her, and, with one hand, he closed the trunk. The other hand slipped slowly up her gown, along the curve of her thighs, feeling her warmth, her hair, the smooth curve of her belly, and following up to her breasts, catching a nipple in his fingers as she turned to him.

"Jimmy." Mary held out the rusty cans of yellow corn as Jimmy lifted her gown and began to finger her breasts. "The little banty. Listen to him crow. Listen."

Jimmy pressed against Mary and said, "Yes, listen." And they both laughed, even as their breath caught and rose and the yellow corn spilled to the ground in a patch of sunlight around their bare feet.

And as Jimmy spread the red plaid shirt on the damp grass next to the yellow corn and lifted Mary's gown over her head, Mary's skin, her smell, her touch, her breath, became everything to Jimmy. It was everything, and yet an everything that made him crazy for more, wanting more and more as he found her breasts, her open thighs, felt her breath moving with his, her moans rising to meet his.

And Jimmy fell with Mary into a time that might have been years, might have been lightning, until his voice rose into the morning, rising past the banty, past the waves breaking and washing again and again on the beach. And Jimmy traveled to the very center of his world.

And when Jimmy lay next to Mary, glistening sweat, breathing the sweet September smells of dried grasses and overripe berries, he fondled Mary's sun-darkened breast as he might a small sacred feather or a smooth round stone from a medicine bundle, remembering the powerful healing magic of its medicine.

The slam of the screen door cracked the air like a shot, and Mary laughed and pulled Jimmy with her as they rolled to the far side of the Buick where they lay and watched the boys tumble off the porch and down the path to the beach with poles and lines and shining cans full of worms.

As Jimmy and Mary dressed, they spoke little, each sensing it was a morning full of a beauty much too sweet and fragile for the weight of words. While Jimmy was buttoning his jeans, he felt Mary brush her hand along his arm and thought he heard her whisper a single line of Uncle's Salish prayer of thanks, but as he turned to see her scoop up the corn and cross the field to the '52 Chev wagon, he wasn't sure if he had heard it or felt it or spoken it himself.

Jimmy carried the water cans and met Mary at the Chev wagon just as the last fat, black-and-white barred rock hens jumped from the open tailgate window, loose feathers and the hot smell of chicken following them in the breeze of flapping wings. And the little banty rooster was surrounded by all his hens, all pecking and scratching and pushing to the center of that sweet yellow corn.

The Indian Rubber Boots

Since Uncle died, Mary had been more quiet than usual. Sometimes Jimmy felt he knew her so well that he could read her like the weather out on the ocean, see all the signs of the storm, the calm, know the direction of the wind. Jimmy felt something in Mary's quiet that he hadn't felt before. Even at the salmon bake for Uncle and the long night of talking and joking around the fire, there was something new in Mary's quiet. It was the sort of quiet that felt like a question, a story gathering in on itself, ready to rise into breath. Tonight, when he felt that same quiet in her after the boys had tumbled and fallen into sleep, Jimmy went alone to the beach and built a fire, wondering if she would follow him.

The fire was burning hot, and enough wood was gathered for a long night when Mary walked the short trail from the cabin to the beach. Neither of them spoke. Jimmy kept his eyes on the fire. But he felt her breath as she first knelt near him and then settled on the blanket next to him.

The moon passed into and through the branches of the madrona above them; the only voice in the night was the clear wash of waves against sand and stone. And when Mary did speak, it seemed a child's tender voice that Jimmy was hearing for the first time, pouring out words as if words were all that existed, all that could fill the wide, dark space between her and the stars. Her voice was so soft, Jimmy could barely breathe, and he felt it as a whisper of warm breath against his cheek.

"There is so much I can't remember, Jimmy. Since Uncle died, all I can remember is that I don't remember. Like a feeling coming into a room after being away for a long time and knowing something is missing, but not being able to tell what it is. All those stories last night, and all I could do is remember what I can't remember.

"I barely remember our first house, the trailer up behind Aunt Lucy's. Our little travel trailer was right behind it, next to it really. That was where we lived, Mother and Dad and Harold and me. It's as if I'm remembering someone else's life, now that they are all gone: first Mother when I was so young, then Dad and Harold going down in the fishing boat, and now Uncle. Funny how I'm thinking about it now.

"But I only remember little things about that time, like waking up once all alone. Everyone was gone. It was after my nap. I started crying and crying, because the stairs down to the yard were too big for me to get down, like they had grown while I was asleep.

"I remember another time sitting on the floor. It was cracked green linoleum. I was eating pieces of fry bread with my baby brother, Harold, and our dog, Frank Sinatra. I'd eat a piece, give a piece to Harold, eat a piece and give a piece to Frank Sinatra. Like that. And Frank Sinatra would bark every time Harold or I would get a turn, and that would make Harold laugh. He got laughing so hard, he got the hiccups and couldn't eat. So Frank Sinatra and I got to finish the rest of that fry bread.

"But mostly, I don't remember too much. I do remember the night the trailer burned down. Though sometimes I think I am remembering what Aunt Lucy told me, she told the story so many times.

"One night Aunt Lucy woke up, right out of her sleep, screaming and shouting. She kept shouting, 'Turn down the burner, turn down the burner.' The stove, the stove. Only in her language: *hudali, hudali.* Anyway, Uncle Arnie knew right away what it was, because Aunt Lucy didn't have any electricity or knobs to turn off in her kitchen. He knew she was seeing something in our trailer, a spirit message in her dreams showing her that danger. Aunt Lucy was always getting messages like that in dreams.

"Well, by the time Uncle got to the trailer, Harold and I were on the steps, crawling down. I was pulling Harold after me by his pajama feet. I do remember that part, being real mad at

Harold. I had heard Aunt Lucy calling me. Sometimes in my dreams, she visited me. She woke me up out of my sleep, she was calling me so loud. In my dream, she was calling and telling me to help her build a fire in her wood cookstove. She was calling me to her, out of the trailer and to her. She said I could have a bowl of huckleberries if I helped. I was hungry and Harold wasn't cooperating. Uncle got to us just as I pulled Harold down the stairs on top of me and we were both heading for the dirt next to the propane tank, the whole trailer becoming smoke behind us.

"The next thing I remember, I was sitting by the warm cookstove and eating that bowl of huckleberries at Aunt Lucy's. I felt safe by that stove. Aunt Lucy was feeding Harold a warm bottle, and Uncle was getting his shoes on to go down to the Tides Inn Tavern to tell Mother and Dad our trailer had burned to the ground. I felt scared. Maybe somehow it was my fault, and they would be mad at me.

"I asked Aunt Lucy, when I was sitting there in her kitchen, eating those huckleberries, to tell me the story of rock *kayə*. I liked to hear her tell it. I didn't want to think about Mother and Dad. She told it in our language, that's when it was best. Some words just don't translate to English. A lot's lost. But the story is good anyway. This is how Aunt Lucy told me the story:

" 'One day an old *kayə*, grandmother, told her grandchildren, I am going down to the water, *ƛuk̓ʷitʼ čəd*. The grandchildren begged and begged their *kayə* to let them come with her. They liked to jump on the wet sand and make the clams squirt water up in the air. The *kayə* was going to the water to dig for *sʔax̌ʷuʔ*, clams, and all those little grandchildren wanted to go with her. The old *kayə* knew that those grandchildren would fuss and fight. But the people were hungry for *sʔax̌ʷuʔ*. So she told her grandchildren, Go get a *sqaləx̌*, a clam digging stick, to help dig *sʔax̌ʷuʔ*. All the grandchildren ran to get a *sqaləx̌* and to meet their *kayə* down at the water's edge. The old *kayə* was already bent over, digging and digging, filling her *x̌ʷʔax̌ʷaʔad*, her basket, with clams. But those grandchildren, they just squirted clams, chased each other with those sticks, and were fighting and fussing. The *kayə* would tell them, Dig clams, help your old *kayə*, but they didn't listen. Well, at that very moment, the Changer just happened to be passing by. He saw those grandchildren fighting and fussing, chasing each other with those *sqaləx̌*, those clam digging sticks, and not listening to their *kayə*, not minding. The Changer didn't like that, those children not minding their *kayə*, and so he changed them all. He changed all those grandchildren into rock crabs, little red rock crabs with the *sqaləx̌* still in their hands. Those little crabs' pinchers, those are their *sqaləx̌*. And that old *kayə*, because she was right there in the middle of the grandchildren when the Changer came by, turned into a big rock. And you look along under that big rock down by the water's edge when the tide is low, and you'll see those little grandchildren forever trying and trying with their *sqaləx̌*, their little pinchers, to help their old *kayə* dig some clams for her basket.'

"That night I wanted Auntie to tell me that story so she'd be right there, talking to me, when my parents got back. I was afraid I'd be in trouble, leaving the trailer to help Auntie with her woodstove, *hudali*, when I was supposed to be asleep, taking care of Harold.

"That's when we moved to town, those years when Mother was so sick. But even then, when I was young, there weren't many of us in town. We moved into a little white house. It was the house built for my Great-Aunt Josephine on her allotment. The edge of her land was where the old village was, down there on the beach, above the rock *kayɔ*. The army tore that down and called it a strategic site and kept it. Later they sold it to a developer. Most of Great-Aunt Josephine's land was lost after she died. I don't know how the little white house was kept. But after Mother died, and then the accident, and I moved back here with Auntie and Uncle, even that house was lost.

"But those years we lived in town, the town wasn't much then. Just a post office, a church, a general store, two taverns, a dance hall, a community center, a small fire station, the old ferry dock, and a little one-room school up on the hill. Funny when I think of it. All those gathering places being built here at the same time that ours were being torn down, covered over, taken away. Imagine that. All the while those folks were building this town, building houses and cabins close together, making it easy to gather, to dance and be social, all up here on the hill, looking down on the beach where even the ashes of the old village had been raked away.

"It was a big change for me and Harold, moving into town.

My parents had white friends. Jim Bob, Al and June, Orville Rogers, like that. Knowing them was natural, just friends. They'd been around. They knew Aunt Lucy and Uncle. They understood. And my dad, he was white. But not white like some of those people in town. Not like Mrs. Larsen—that's what we weren't used to.

"Mrs. Larsen was our next-door neighbor. She was Swedish and kept her hair always wrapped up in those gray braids that went around and around her head. Harold and I used to make up stories about those snakes on her head, sucking her brains up, stuff like that.

"Everybody in town called Mrs. Larsen the Swedish Cookie Lady. We weren't Lutherans, so we never tasted them. If we went to church at all, we would go to the Catholic church. Though after they wouldn't bury Great-Aunt Josephine because she had attended Shaker meetings with her brother's wife, Dad wouldn't let us go to church much. But we could always smell those cookies baking. Mrs. Larsen wouldn't give us any unless we went to the Lutheran Sunday school, I remember. Me and Harold went to her house and asked her if we could each taste one cookie, and that's what she told us. I really remember smelling those cookies at times when my mother wasn't baking much. She was sick with the TB then, though I didn't really know it, and me and Harold would get so hungry with that smell of those cookies baking, we'd try to make some. We'd mix up a bunch of stuff and cook it, but we never did make anything worth eating.

"And Mrs. Larsen's yard was always full of plants and flowers we'd never seen. Something was always blooming, even in the middle of winter. But anytime wild blackberry or salal tried to grow in her yard, she'd be out there hacking or spraying.

"Sometimes Mrs. Larsen would ask Dad to help her. She'd need something heavy moved, some wood chopped or some shrub dug up, and she'd ask him. But the way she said it, I remember, always sounded like she was doing this nice favor for him, helping him. And instead of money, she'd give him some old thing, a coffeepot with a broken lid, a chair with the cane split off, a box of half-rotten apples. Well, he wasn't doing it to get that old stuff, that's for sure. He was just being neighborly.

"Once she gave him a big box of her old housedresses, telling him that my mother needed some decent clothes to do housework in. Any picture of my mother will show you that she knew how to dress. She was always sewing something on that treadle sewing machine in the living room. I know that sometimes, when she couldn't buy fabric, she'd use old drapes and men's wool suits and white dress shirts and come up with the latest fashion, shoulder pads, brass buttons, and all. But that box of old housedresses never made it into the house. Dad went straight to the backyard, stuck them in the burn barrel, and lit them on fire.

"Mrs. Larsen wasn't too happy when we moved in. I know she didn't like having me and Harold and HolyMary and Jesus make noise and run through her yard. HolyMary and Jesus were our chickens. HolyMary was a white leghorn. Jesus was a Rhode Island Red rooster. Our Uncle Henry gave them to me and Harold when Dad drove us all out to our relations on the Makah reservation on the coast for a visit. Harold and I told Dad we wanted really important names for our chickens, not regular names like Aunt Lucy's chickens Ramona, Agnes, and all those names of Uncle's old girlfriends. That always made us laugh, hearing Aunt Lucy talk about chasing Ramona or eating Agnes or plucking Sophie. Aunt Lucy liked to talk about those chickens like that, until Harold and I could almost believe they were Uncle's girlfriends running around the yard. But we wanted more important names. And of all the names Dad told us, HolyMary and Jesus sounded the most important. And, of course, I thought that Holy was a proper name, like Mrs. Smith or something, a way to tell her from me, his little Mary. That's what he called me, My Little Mary, like it was a title.

"We just let HolyMary and Jesus run loose, like we did at Aunt Lucy's. They didn't have the company of Aunt Lucy's chickens anymore, but they did okay. HolyMary found a good nesting spot up under the back porch. Harold and I would always be under that porch checking for an egg. And there was plenty for HolyMary and Jesus to eat, slugs, bugs, whatnot like that, up and down the block. If they went too far from home, we'd just holler HolyMary and Jesus, and they'd come running home.

"We never really worried about HolyMary and Jesus, because they were smart and could run fast to get away from children and dogs. They were used to that at Aunt Lucy's, that's for sure. And then Dad rigged up a wooden cross in the backyard, next to Mrs. Larsen's rosebushes, for a roost. It makes me laugh to think of that now, that old cross with Jesus just crowing away there in the morning.

"The first time Mrs. Larsen ever spoke to us, she told my mother that her children's horrible little fowl were leaving their little calling cards all over her front lawn and they would have to stop. Well, first we had to figure out what she was talking about. I mean, who has calling cards on the reservation? Either you're there or you're not. You don't need a card to tell you that.

"Dad didn't make things any better when he went over and told Mrs. Larsen if she wanted HolyMary and Jesus to quit shitting in her yard to just say it in English. We could tell he was holding his temper in when he told her that. She kept her blinds pulled for three days after that.

"Whenever something came up about us bothering Mrs. Larsen, Dad would just tell us to stay away, leave her alone. We knew he didn't like her, but he still wanted us to behave. I think he just didn't want to think about her.

"Dad moved HolyMary and Jesus' cross to the far side of the yard, next to the vacant lot, and HolyMary and Jesus got so they liked the blackberries and woods best anyway. He put Frank Sinatra on a run, in the daytime, next to Mrs. Larsen's roses. HolyMary and Jesus weren't fond of Frank Sinatra, and Frank Sinatra made it his job to keep HolyMary and Jesus away from Mrs. Larsen. He'd howl every time they got too near.

"Even with HolyMary and Jesus under control, Mrs. Larsen wasn't too happy with me and Harold. I think she spent all her time watching us to find something she could be irritated about. She was always picking up our stuff and dumping it on our porch. Rocks, sticks, sock-balls, string, whatever we played with and left by her yard or even down the street or in the woods behind us. She'd spend her time doing that just to prove something about me and Harold, I guess. It couldn't have been much, 'cause we never had the money for real toys. Harold had a horsie, General Dwight D. Eisenhower the Horse, but he made that out of an old half-circle piece of green hose, and he kept General Dwight D. Eisenhower tied up at the back porch with an old boot lace. The only time General Dwight D. Eisenhower the Horse got off the back porch was when Harold was riding him. I only got to ride General Dwight D. Eisenhower once.

"Harold let me ride his horse the day he was making a secret code machine with an old mirror. I guess he wanted me out of his way. So I rode General Dwight D. Eisenhower around the house, up and down the block, and right along the very edge of Mrs. Larsen's little flowers in the front by the road. I could see her watching me from her living room window making sure I didn't touch any.

"Well, the secret code machine must not have worked, because when Harold called me he had little pieces of that mirror all tied onto a couple of box tops for secret enemy stun-guns, instead. We spent the rest of the afternoon standing by Mrs. Larsen's back hedge, making those little mirror pieces catch that sun, sending it into Mrs. Larsen's window. When she came to the window, we'd hide in the hedge and pet Frank Sinatra, our trusty military intelligence dog, and as soon as she'd look away, we'd start up again. It was just something to do. Being kids, I guess, we thought of those things.

"Dad got home late that night from the woods. He was on a logging crew out by Forks then, and he'd be gone a week or two at a time. That night, even before he got his boots off or got his first beer, here comes Mrs. Larsen. She had Harold's horse in her hand, and even before she got up the steps, she was telling Dad how Harold and I were making the sun come into her house and hurt her eyes. She said that his dirty Indian children even broke the end off one of the branches of her prized laurel hedge, and then she huffed off down the steps back to her house and slammed her door.

"Dad's chain saw was on the floor by his feet, his thirty-six-inch Stihl, still covered with sawdust. He looked at that saw and then at Mother. He told Mother that maybe he should fix Mrs. Larsen's goddamned prized laurel hedge for her so she wouldn't have to worry about any more dirty Indian children's fingers touching it again. That way Mrs. Larsen would never have to wonder where the sun came from, either.

"Well, Mother and Dad got to laughing and laughing about how they could scare Mrs. Larsen good, something to make

Jesus and HolyMary's calling cards look like mint candy gifts in comparison. And now, thinking about it, I can see Mother smiling and saying, 'Oh, no, Ed, you'd better not,' but all the time holding the door, handing him his favorite knit cap.

"Harold and I went running to the kitchen window and pressed our noses up to the glass. Mother had her hands on our shoulders, just laughing and saying, 'Oh, Ed, oh, Ed.' Her voice sounded as happy as any time I can remember. In that little light from the back porch we could just see Dad out there in the night next to Mrs. Larsen's laurel hedge. He started up his saw and goosed it real loud. It sounded louder than any saw in the woods. We'd never heard it there in the backyard before, and it felt like the whole house was shaking. It was an exciting moment. Our dad was not afraid of Mrs. Larsen after all. He just kept goosing it, walking up and down and up and down that hedge, like he was cutting. We could see Mrs. Larsen's house light up like a church. Dad gunned the saw even more. But she never came out.

"That pretty much took care of Mrs. Larsen and her complaining. After that, she had a little square greenhouse built on the other side of her lot, and she spent most nice days in there. She kept to herself after that.

"All this time, of course, was right before Mother died from TB. She must have been sick all the time we were in that white house in town. But I didn't know it then. I've got that one picture that my Uncle Charles gave me of all of us then, and I can see it, in her eyes. It's a sad picture, really. But I guess I thought my mother was still young and beautiful. Maybe children don't always see the truth of their parents' lives.

"I try sometimes to remember my mother. But it is only bits and pieces of our lives that I remember: the trailer, Uncle and Auntie, Jesus and HolyMary, Harold's horsie, Mrs. Larsen, Dad and his chain saw. Little things like that.

"Maybe if somebody had told me then, when I was a young girl, This is important, now pay attention, then maybe I'd be able to tell more, to remember my own mother.

"One time does come clear to me. It makes me sad. It's just a little thing, but it makes me so sad.

"I have to tell you first, though, that the one thing I know about my mother is that she was a good swimmer. Everybody knew that about her. Her friends talk about her swimming across to the island.

"That and the Christmas party she gave at Aunt Lucy's house in July. That's a long story, but I will just tell you that one year she went visiting in the winter all the houses of all her good friends. I was a baby so I went, too. And she'd come in and say she just stopped for coffee. Of course everybody loved my mother and loved to visit with her. Well, while they were getting her coffee, she'd slip some little thing, an ashtray, a lighter, a sewing thimble, into her pocket. She even managed to get a couple of sweaters, a pillow, and a framed family photo. Pretty soon she had something from everybody, some special little thing. In the summer she called a big party for all her friends, had Dad dress up as Santa Claus right in the middle of July. He carried out this big old sack with all those little things she'd collected all winter. She'd wrapped them all up, real pretty, and handed them out to who they belonged to. Sort of a Christmas in July. Giveaway, I guess, or maybe you'd call it a get-back. Well, most people thought that was the funniest thing ever, getting their own missing things back like that, all wrapped up at this party. But there were some that didn't think it was funny, and still don't, and they're the ones that don't tell me anything about Mother.

"But the ones that do, the ones that liked her party, they're the ones that like to talk about her swimming across to the island. She really could swim. She knew the water, knew just when to go, how to stay out of those currents. She couldn't get anyone to cross with her, in that cold water. She'd swim alone, over to the island, rest on the hot sand, and then, when the tide was right again, she'd swim back.

"Uncle gave her the name $\check{x}^w \acute{u} \check{x} \partial y \,?$, Little Diving Bird. $\check{x}^w \acute{u} \check{x} \partial y \,?$ was heron's wife. Uncle and his friends used to see my mother diving and swimming way out in the bay alone and, sure enough, there on the shore would be a skinny-legged boy waiting for her: $sb \partial \acute{q}^w a \,?$, heron, waiting for $\check{x}^w \acute{u} \check{x} \partial y \,?$ to return, just like those old stories. And that's how some people still remember her, as $\check{x}^w \acute{u} \check{x} \partial y \,?$, Little Diving Bird.

"But she must have been sick when we were in that little

white house in town, because she never even taught Harold and me to swim. And we never even saw her swim once.

"The day I think of now is the only day I can remember going to the beach with her. There was only a little bit of beach left below the town, between all those summer cabins, where we were allowed to go. It used to be part of the beach where people gathered, dug clams, and lived together. But it was only that little beach then. And of course, when the white man came he brought his whiskey and his garbage. And so then, everyone was drinking and dirtying their beach there. When my mother was young she used to run the whole beach, but for me and Harold, it was just that little strip, full of broken glass. Maybe we went more, there is a lot I don't remember. I just remember that once.

"There were other kids and mothers at the beach, nobody we knew. Kids in the water, mothers on the *gʷistaləb,* sand. Everybody was in their bathing suits. Harold and I had our bathing suits on, too. But mother made us wear those rubber boots. Half our life barefoot, and then we go to the beach and we have to wear rubber boots. Mine were red and Harold's were blue, and along the top of each of our boots were those cartoonlike Indians with tomahawks and big noses and a feather sticking out of the top of their heads, and they were chasing each other around and around the tops of our boots. The other kids there had sandals. We couldn't afford sandals, I guess. So she made us wear those boots to protect us from our own beach. She called them our Indian Rubber Boots, like it was a title or a proper name. The Indian Rubber Boots. Harold and I found them once after Mother had died. We burned them in a little pit we dug out next to HolyMary and Jesus' cross perch.

"And, you know, the last time I remember seeing my mother was with Harold and my dad. We were standing outside, somewhere I'd never been. It was a cold, clear day. February. And we were all bundled up in our coats standing outside of a tall white wall. And Dad said, 'There's your mother, wave at your mother.' I couldn't figure out what he meant, all I see is this tall white wall. And he pointed way up that wall for me and Harold. And we looked up and saw this little window with this face in it and a hand, waving and waving. That was my mother. Oh. I don't like to remember that, it makes me feel so bad, thinking of that mother up in that window, that father and those little children out in the cold, looking up to her.

"But for a long time, after Mother died, when someone at school would call me an Indian, I'd think of the Indian Rubber Boots. And I'd think they'd seen me on that beach in those boots. And I'd think of that feeling, those hot boots, full of sand, rubbing my legs red and raw around the top where the Indians were chasing each other. I'd say I was not an Indian. I knew Auntie always called us *ʔacittalbix*ʷ. But I'd be so mad at my mother for making us wear those boots, making people think I was one of those Indians running around and around, chasing each other with tomahawks, that I'd deny them all. All my ancestors and relations. Oh, I get so sad thinking about those boots, about how much that hurt, about saying I wasn't an Indian. I get sad. I suppose I shouldn't. It's such a little thing, a little part of a story, really. But I still do feel sad.

"I wish there was more. But eight years with my mother and that's what I remember, those boots. The Indian Rubber Boots: *pastəd stk̓ʷabsəd,* white man's shoes."

Mary rolled into Jimmy's arms, and he held her, combing the moonlight into her hair with his fingers, while she cried softly and whispered over and over, "I don't even know why I'm crying."

Missionaries
and Soldiers

The air had been still and heavy and hot all day at the net sheds. But now there was a soft breeze coming off the water. From where Jimmy stood on the dock, working on repairing the last of the lines, he could see Roy silhouetted against the dark of the Olympic Mountains at the horizon. The mountains were turning a deep blue-black, but the sky was still bright, the color of burnished abalone. Jimmy shivered, maybe from the breeze, maybe from the perfect beauty of that evening.

Jimmy's hands were rough and bleeding in places. Already, in these short weeks, his hands had lost the callused hardness they had built up handling nets, cables, line, and the tons of salmon they pulled in off Neah Bay and north. But what the skin of his hands had forgotten, his legs and body remembered, swaying even now at the sound of the waves lapping at the creosote pilings under the dock where they stood.

"I should be getting my car in the morning." Roy's fingers worked as he spoke, twisting and knotting the line. Roy had an easy way, in whatever work he did, of making it look like he wasn't really working. But when the day was over, it always seemed that Roy's stack or pile was greater, whether it was clams or fish or nets or kindling or fry bread. Something about his steadiness, Jimmy thought, a steadiness that some people mistook for slowness.

"What car, Roy? You didn't tell me about no car."

"When you were back up at the shed, getting the last of the nets, I saw Cousin George. You remember that Malibu of his, the one he won off that poor sucker in that poker game last year?"

"Sure do."

"Well, when he brought it home, the Flo-Lows were up at his place right away trying to buy it off of him. He didn't want to sell it, so I just said, 'George, when you fuck it up, can I have it,' and he says, 'Sure.' So he just came by here a few minutes ago and says, 'Well, Roy, I fucked it up, you still want it?' " Roy and Jimmy laughed. "Yeah, don't know if I can drive it away or if I'll have to borrow Flo-Low's truck to haul it over."

"Have you seen it?"

"Not yet, but I've heard about it."

"That bad, huh?"

"Well, Flo-Low told me what happened to it last winter. I guess it was a bad winter here. Anyway, Cousin George drove to Seattle during one of the cold spells, and he got so drunk he forgot he had his car. He was on one of his benders, and by the time he came around, he had to wait another week to even re-member he had a car. But there was a foot of snow on the ground. When he finally got back to his car, a couple of winos had moved in, trying to get out of that snow and cold. The guys living in it were nice enough. Cousin George even knew one of their cousins from Makah. But Flo-Low said they tore the hell out of the inside trying to keep warm. Guess it smelled like a urinal in an old bar. The seats were pretty much gone, and there were a couple of burns on the floor in the back where they lit some Sterno cans. So I've been listening to the stories, watching that Malibu, piece by piece, get fucked up."

And Jimmy's mind stepped back to the night on the beach after Uncle died, the night that Lucy cooked them salmon and clams, and the stories that flowed all night, as though a dam had broken, when even Cousin George, usually good for a quick story that would leave them all laughing, stories of fishing, of women, started talking. Around the fire George began, as all the men had that night, as if the words were the threads that would bind them all together and attach them to a memory of Uncle like an anchor.

"I moved to this place when I was eighteen. Well, actually, you might say I moved back. My parents and Gramps had moved away while I was in the Job Corps. I moved in alone when I got back. So I always think of that time as when I moved in.

"Not that I don't think of living here while I was growing up. I do. But being a kid in a house is different from being on your own. So when I think of this place when I was growing up, living with my folks and Gramps and everybody that lived around here, I think of it differently. Like it was somewhere else.

"I think memory is like that. You can be in one place, and you can remember it at the same time, like it's really two places, but all the time it's one. Just layers and layers of years peeling away, I guess. Until you find things that sort of come back to you, clear as day, if you let them. Sometimes, watching this place change, seeing people leave and die and all these new people coming in who don't know shit, the remembering keeps me from going crazy.

"So those two years in the Job Corps are like a big black band for me, separating the time I was a kid here from being here now.

"The first time I ever rode in an airplane was when I left from Seattle to the Job Corps. I'll tell you now, flying is totally weird. I look at those big hunks of metal and think, There's no way that that thing is going to go flying through the air a million miles up.

"But we got up in the air, and I'm about petrified, white knuckles, sweating, and here's these stewardesses all dolled up in lipstick and red fingernails and puffed-up bleached-out hair.

"And what I want is to be strapped in, buckled up in an asbestos suit, a metal helmet, a parachute, and constant emergency instructions over the loudspeaker. I want flight attendants that look like fighter pilots, not cream puffs.

"And then, the whole trip, the voice of the fucking pilot comes on and tells us to look out the window to see this town or that mountain or this river. Shit, I was so scared I thought I'd die. I don't like to even get up on a ladder. I wasn't going to look out no fucking window way the hell up there.

"When I finally got out of the plane, I thought I'd landed in some foreign country, I'll tell you. I'd spent most of my life on the beach and in the woods, and then I fly through space in some bullet-shaped trailer and get out in the middle of nowhere.

"I'll tell you, it was the fucking middle of nowhere, and all I've got is one duffel bag and five bucks from Job Corps for a taxi. That taxi ride had me about as scared as the plane ride. When I heard that the Job Corps was twenty miles from the airport, I thought there's no way I could walk twenty miles in the middle of the fucking desert, and I sure as hell didn't know how you got a taxi. I mean, I almost didn't go to the Job Corps, worrying about that twenty miles.

"But the Job Corps said they'd have a taxi waiting for me and even sent me the five bucks. They paid for everything then, plane tickets, bus tickets, taxi fare, whatever you needed. I guess they didn't want to lose any of us sniffly nosed underage kids coming from all the hell over the country. Just imagine if they'd lost one of us.

"So when I get there, there's this taxi waiting for me. This Mexican. Now, don't get me wrong. I don't care about him being Mexican, his brown skin or any of that shit. Hell, my own mother's mother was supposed to have some Portuguese blood in with the Indian. Never really have even gotten a straight answer on what tribe. Things get so screwed up. People hiding what they are, trying so hard to protect their kids from whatever suffering they had in their life. And then the kids start to figure it out, think they've been lied to. Can get your mind pretty messed up. Just claim what you can, honor that, I guess.

"Anyway, my mother had black curly hair, brown as any Mexican. My dad was a blue-eyed Norwegian, which makes me kind of a bleach job, I guess. I don't usually say anything. Oh, somebody's always asking me in the middle of winter how I got so tanned, if I went to Hawaii or some damn place like that. I used to just say I was Indian, not explaining all of it or anything like that, and that would shut them up. Once this guy said something about there must of been a Swede in the wood-pile. The dumb bastard couldn't tell a Norwegian from a Swede and he was crazy enough to open his big mouth so I beat the crap out of him. Nowadays, I just usually don't say anything. Nobody's fucking business, as far as I can see.

"But this guy, this Mexican taxi driver, I was as glad to get out of that taxi as I was getting out of that plane. For twenty miles I had to listen to him tell me how his wife was so mean, so sick, and how much he liked strong, healthy boys like me, until I thought I'd about puke. When that taxi stopped I threw that five bucks over the seat and shot out of there like a bat out of hell, with him calling after me about wanting just a little feel.

"So there I was in Texas, Land of Sam Houston Days. I think about that, where they'd dig a big hole, build a fire, throw in a couple of cows and cover it back up with a bulldozer and cook it a couple days. First time I went to one of those things, a big guy asked me if I was hungry, and when I told him I was, he handed me a shovel and said help myself. Now, I'd been to a clam bake, but never anywhere they'd baked a whole fucking cow.

"It all looked the same to me, Texas, all that godforsaken land, miles and miles of it. Drive along for hours and wouldn't see nothing, and then out in the middle of nowhere there'd be this old square ice house converted into a bar. Two quarts of the stuff down there and you'd be drunk on your ass.

"When it came time for me to leave, Job Corps gave me a plane ticket home. Well, I'd ridden that plane down, and I'd had enough of that shit. And besides, I had all this stuff stored up, shit I'd stolen, clothes, duffel bags, machinery, pants, and this '57 Caddy I was working on.

"I heard they'd give you a bus ticket instead of a plane ticket, so I thought that was my chance. They got you door to door, since they were responsible for you, so when I got my bus ticket, this guy takes me to the bus station and drops me off.

"Hell, I just hid in the bathroom until the bus left, and I pocketed the ticket and got myself an apartment so I could get a job, fix up the car, and drive all that stuff I'd been collecting home to Washington.

"Well, shit, I was ten months from being eighteen. I'd never thought of that. Nobody would hire me as a mechanic until I was eighteen. All that training in the Job Corps and the only place I could work was a fucking gas station. Ten hours a day, seven days a week. Seventy-five bucks. Could hardly pay the rent for that.

"But I did it for a little while. I still had all the Job Corps clothes, those uniforms, so when I'd get hungry I'd just go over and chow down. Nobody checked or anything. I'd just eat a mess of food, go home until I got hungry next time, and then I'd go back over.

"Finally, the car broke down, blew the transmission, and I got sick of Texas. It was summer and hotter than hell out there. So I decided to get out of that godforsaken place.

"I just locked up the apartment with all that stuff I'd been collecting still inside and threw away the key. I washed the car and left the key to it on the seat and called a taxi.

"Shit. I couldn't believe it. I was hardly out of the phone booth and who pulls up in the taxi but that same joker, that Mexican who brought me to the Job Corps in the first place.

"If I hadn't of been so sick of Texas, I'd have called another taxi. But I sure as hell wanted to get the fuck out of that place, so I figured, I can handle this guy now. So I throw in my bag, and before I can even get my ass on the seat he starts up again. Same old line. Mean, sick wife, he likes boys. Must have run it off to everybody in pants who got in his taxi. Guess it worked enough times for him to keep it up.

"I pretty much ignored him this time, except I thought I'd about puke listening to him go on about how much he liked boys, their soft little cheeks, shit like that.

"So we get to the bus station, and he makes it clear that it's five bucks for the ride, unless I want to let him have a little feel, then the ride, so to speak, is on him. I just ignored the guy.

"But when I go to get out, he says, 'Can I carry your bags?' Hell, all I had was this little duffel bag, must have weighed three pounds, max. I just says, 'No, I don't want you to carry my fucking bag.' And I go to pay him, and he starts up about what I can do instead of giving him that five bucks.

"I give him the five bucks, and then he says, 'How about a little tip, just a little feel at least.' He made it real clear he always got tips.

"Well, I'd had it with that fruitcake. So I says, 'Sure, I'll give you a tip,' and I leaned over and reached in the window and grabbed him by the collar and pulled him over and bashed his head against the door a couple of times. Knocked him senseless, I think. I don't know, I didn't stick around.

"I ran as fast as I could to that bus station. And I got the hell out of Texas.

"But we weren't gone more than twenty minutes, maybe thirty, and this big old hundred-pound suitcase comes flying off the luggage rack and smashes down on this guy sleeping right across from me. Smashed him good. Landed right on his skull.

"It might have killed him, but I never did find out, because when we pulled into the next station just down the road, there is this whole shitload of cop cars, and I thought, oh God, they're coming to get me now.

"So I went clear to the back of the bus and stayed down real low in my seat. Most of the other people got off and watched them carry off the guy with the suitcase on his head. Not me, I stayed low, hoping nobody'd figure I was the guy who'd smashed up the Mexican fruitcake taxi driver. We were in that little nothing of a town for hours waiting before we left, me all scrunched down the back, still figuring that they were after me for smacking that cab driver.

"When we finally got going again, I thought we'd just head north, a straight shot. But, hell, we stopped in every podunk town between here and Texas. Seven of the fucking longest days of my life were spent on that bus. Have you ever smelled the inside of a bus for seven days?

"I swore I'd never get on a bus again after that trip. Haven't either. Well, one city bus. But after a block, I said, 'Let me off this goddamned thing,' and I got out and walked.

"Well, when I finally got to Poulsbo, all I had left was one dime. I stood there with that dime, looking at the phone booth, and thought, What if I get a wrong number? What if Gramps answers? Shit, Gramps was about deaf. The only thing he could hear was the fucking telephone. After he'd pick it up, he'd just say Hello, Hello, about a million times, and you could be screaming at him, and he'd just be saying Hello, Hello, until he'd finally hang up the phone. I knew I didn't want to spend my last dime on Gramps saying Hello, Hello. So I spent it on cigarettes and walked the ten miles out to our place.

"A dark fucking night, I remember that. And when I got home, the place is empty. Doors wide open. Phone was gone even. Took me a few days to find out where they'd gone. My folks never were letter writers; I wasn't too good at letters myself then. And they just never thought of calling or telling anyone, I guess. And it wasn't like there was a greeting committee there to meet me, to sort of fill me in on what was going on.

"But it was home to me, so I stayed. That was years ago now, I guess. So you can maybe see why I think of the Job Corps, that trip to Texas, as being the black line that separated being at this place from being here now. I was talking to Uncle about a month ago, before the sickness set in bad. He told me a story about his grandfather, Frank Moses, walking out to some lake, miles from here, over toward the mountains, I'd guess, and how he had some journey, falling down to the bottom of the freezing lake, taking him to a place in another world that you can only get to from the bottom of the lake, some scary shit like that. He came back a different person, knowing what he was supposed to do. Went as a boy. Came back a man. But with just a little something more. Thinking about that story used to scare the shit out of me. But lately, in a weird fucking way, I've been thinking that getting on that airplane, flying through space to Texas, the cab rides, all of it, it was the same to me as that weird trip of Uncle's grandfather. It was the black line separating then from now."

Jimmy threw Roy the end of the line. Roy turned slightly to catch it, and when he did, he saw a man leaning on the rail at the top of the ramp that led down to the dock where they stood. A tug had just pulled into the harbor and tied up at the last slip. The wake from the tug hit the docks, sending up the creaking sounds of wood against wood as the docks and piling and boats shifted and rose and fell. Though Jimmy and Roy were moving on the dock, it looked to Roy as if the man on the ramp were leaping up and down into the evening sky.

"See that man up there?" said Roy.

Jimmy turned to look.

"He was down here a while ago when Cousin George was giving me his fucked-up car, and he just sort of stepped into our conversation."

"He got a fucked-up car for you, too?"

"No, but it seems that he had a Malibu once, like Cousin George's, made us practically blood brothers, I guess."

"What—he want to buy Cousin George's Malibu off you already?"

"No, he just wanted to suck up. You know, let us know he

knew we were Indians, and that he'd met some of us before and really liked us."

"Oh, shit." Jimmy laughed. "Another Friend of the Indian."

"Yeah. Seems that he'd driven his Malibu all over some Indian reservation. Took him a whole day to get from one side to the other." Roy laughed. "Yeah, Flo-Low looked at him real serious and says, 'Yeah, I had a car like that once, too.' But the guy didn't much get it, started asking us if we were Indian fishermen. Hell, Cousin George and Flo-Low and I finally had to go sit in the boat for a while to get away from his questions."

Jimmy looked again at the figure silhouetted against the pale yellows and blues of the evening sky. The sun had been down long enough now for the mountains to take on the black of night. The docks were quiet except for the tug crew. Jimmy had heard bits and pieces of their conversation as they got ready for a night of drinking, and he thought he heard the captain, Lars, say "Fucking Indins, fucking lazy goddamned Indins." Jimmy tried to ignore the tug, but he kept his head turned just enough to keep it in sight. He'd heard of Lars, of the fights, of how his wife left him after he came back from Vietnam last spring, half crazy, drinking, threatening her, hitting her around. All Jimmy had ever seen of Lars was nights like this, tying up the tug after a trip, being loud, drinking, and finally going up the ramp and into the Tides Inn. Jimmy had overheard in a conversation on the docks that Lars was better since his wife left him, that living with a woman like her, tight jeans that wouldn't stay home when he was gone, would make any man crazy. But Jimmy hadn't noticed any change.

The sounds from the tugboat were muffled as the crew went into the wheelhouse. Jimmy could hear the swoop of a nighthawk over the grass field up from the beach. He watched as the silhouette of the man on the ramp darkened with the night, and he watched the man's head seeming to bob in and out of the letter *V* of the Tides Inn Tavern sign across the gravel road from the docks.

The old gravel road ran along the beach. It was a short stretch of road going nowhere, never joining into any other road. At either end it narrowed into winding paths down to the beach. Behind the tavern, fishermen and boat owners could drive through the parking lot to get to that gravel road and move their gear closer to the docks and the one small, steep, uneven launching ramp.

Sometimes, along the quarter of a mile of the road nearest the docks and the beach, a few trucks would be parked and nets spread out next to makeshift sheds. One of these sheds had been Uncle's, and it was left now to Jimmy and Roy and their cousins George and Flo-Low.

Jimmy and Roy had helped Uncle build it the first summer they came out to visit from Oklahoma. They walked the beaches and scavenged the lumber and timbers and the creosote footings the same way Uncle built an addition onto his cabin. With the lumber mill and creosote plant across the bay and all the summer people tossing out the leftovers from building their cabins along the beach, there was always plenty of material. It took some looking and some work at hauling it down the beach, but on any day something could be found. Two-by-fours, beams, shakes, shingles, end bolts, rolls of tar paper, and boxes of nails. It just took a little imagination to put it all together.

Jimmy and Roy had been young, energetic, and glad to be on this adventure, in this place so foreign to Oklahoma, and Uncle understood that. And they did as fine a job as anyone on that shed. They covered the whole shed with cedar shakes, roof and sides, split from the cedar ends that were cast out at the mill. It was fine, clear, straight-grain cedar that split like butter and hooked them like popcorn. It was a ploy, Jimmy understood now, since they ended up splitting more cedar shakes and covering Uncle's cabin and roofing Aunt Lucy's, too. Probably that was all Uncle really wanted in the first place. But Uncle understood young men's pride. He understood the importance of mastering and building something alone, even if it was a net shed.

All these years later the shed stood, leaning, sun-bleached silver gray, spilling over with nets and equipment, as a testimony to their youthful passion and as a legacy of their early apprenticeship with Uncle. And like the other sheds, it stood as a healing, a recovery, a reclamation from what this road had once meant to Uncle and his cousins and friends.

Where the tavern stood now, Jimmy knew that the last long-house had been built. He had seen a photo of the scorched longhouse timbers. All around there were young Indian men in suits. One was posing with a baseball bat in his hands. Next to him was a young, dark woman in Sunday clothes, black hair pinned up. And behind the people in the picture were thin-walled, white tents that had been set up by the same army that had burned down their longhouse. The first wooden houses were being nailed up on the logged-off hill. Shortly after that photo was taken, the Indian Agency and the church were built on the ashes of the longhouse.

Uncle knew all the people in the picture. He had been a young man when the army had burned the longhouse. They were told that the burning was to stop diseases from spreading. But it was clear that the reason was to keep them from gathering, to separate them onto allotments, to get them to church. The summer the picture was taken, a police boat came and rounded up all the children over the age of three, taking them up the sound with the children of other tribes to a government school for Indians. Their hair was cut, they wore starched, high-collared uniforms, they were beaten if they spoke their own language. The boys were taught to be mechanics, and the girls worked in the kitchen or the laundry.

The picture was taken before the road was built. And with the road came the jail, another addition off the back of the Indian Agency. It wouldn't take much to get Uncle and his friends to remember what crime, what fight, what night of drinking it was that sentenced them to hard labor along that road, clearing, pulling stumps, hauling sand and rocks up from the beach. Given the choice of jail or hard labor, it wasn't too hard to choose labor. They knew they'd always have good company on the road. So it was their crimes and their labor that built the docks, the Indian Agency, the church, and, foot by foot, a road that went nowhere.

Sometimes Jimmy saw those net sheds along that bit of road as the longhouse in disguise, a place where young men gathered with their elders, heard the stories, understood where they had come from, learned and practiced the skills they needed to be men in the world they were cast into. A place to swap stories and lies. Jimmy was lost in memory of the stories, the laughter that kept them all alive, all coming back to this place, until the voices on the tug grew louder and broke the quiet evening.

Somebody called out, "Hey Indian. Salmon Breath."

Somebody else yelled, "Indian boy, you better get home to your little Pocahontas because Lars here, he likes red meat." Drunken laughter followed, and the voices faded back into the night.

Jimmy looked at Roy, and Roy gestured back up to the ramp.

"Looks like we're going to have a little company too," said Roy.

The vapor light on the dock, above where Roy and Jimmy worked, had come on in the growing darkness, centering them now in the yellow glow of its circle. Just outside the circle, Jimmy could see a figure coming down the ramp.

"I think we're in for it now," Roy whispered. "I've only got this little bit to go. Can you listen to him that long?"

"Oh, hell, yes," said Jimmy. "A few minutes of The Friend of the Indian won't kill me."

"Howdy, there." The man entered their circle of light. He had slicked-down light brown hair and was wearing new blue jeans and a short black car coat and new white boat shoes. "You two have been working so hard, I thought I might join you here, see what it is you're up to."

Jimmy and Roy kept working, fingers sliding and twisting and tying line. Jimmy always thought this last little bit of work they did on the line at the docks was his best. Even though it was cramped, somehow he felt that the sound of the waves on the pilings, the steady bump and crunch of the boats as they rose and fell against the dock, and the smell of the water and the salt breeze, all of this got into his fingers, kept the rhythm. Like dancing to a good band, when you didn't even have to think to know how your body should move. Maybe the dancing to the drums and rattles at the longhouse had been like that. But Jimmy's thoughts were interrupted.

"The name's Andrews. Andy Andrews. Don't think I introduced myself when I talked to you earlier. You two have been putting in a long day."

Jimmy didn't look at Roy, but he wanted to. He knew Roy was thinking what he was thinking: Us Indians all look alike. In fact, two Indians in the evening are just the same as three in the afternoon. Maybe better.

"I hope I'm not bothering you. I don't mean to bother, just wanted to say howdy, see what you're doing."

Jimmy started softening, feeling sorry for the guy. He probably didn't know shit about fishing, was lonely and just wanted somebody to talk to. Jimmy had met harmless guys like him before, sort of pathetic, really. They worked all week, maybe even some weekends, in some dark little office in the city. When they came out to the docks for a day, it was as if they'd stepped out of a cave after forty years. You could almost see them blinking, amazed that a whole world of people was living and breathing outside of that cave.

Once, back in Oklahoma, when Jimmy was younger and Grandma One Rock was still alive, Jimmy had watched as an earnest young man, a tourist, who had been hanging around a tribal gathering all weekend, talking and laughing too loudly, finally joined in a Stomp Dance at night, dancing with awkward, overly exaggerated gestures. Jimmy and Roy came alongside, making jokes and imitating him.

They didn't see Grandma One Rock as she came up and stood behind them. She only said, He must need to be here, there is some reason, something he needs to honor. You boys just let him dance, give him food, and stay out of his way. He must need to be here. Jimmy remembered wondering if Grandma One Rock believed her own words. But sometimes, meeting guys like that, trying so hard to be Indian, to be something they didn't know shit about, he thought about what Grandma One Rock said and let them be.

"Oh, we're just patching up the old nets, fixing this last line here, and getting ready to head out in the morning."

"You fishermen?"

Roy pointed to Uncle's boat. "That's our boat there. We'll be going out in the morning."

"You know, I've had a house near Puget Sound most of my life and not ever been on a fishing boat."

"That so," said Roy.

"Traveled all over. I was in mission work for a while. Couple of years ago I was in Polynesia for six months. Now that's some place. Friendliest natives you'd ever want to meet. Take to the Lord like a cat to milk, too. I went out fishing many a time with them. But a whole different operation there."

"That so," said Roy.

"You can say that again. Now, over there, instead of these big heavy gasoline boats, they've got these little boats they make. And their nets. Totally different."

The man in the short black coat reached out and grabbed the net, upsetting Jimmy's rhythm, knocking the bone needle out of his hands. It was an old one of Uncle's. It dropped, hit the line, and bounced off into the water. Roy dropped to his knees, plucking it from the water before it drifted out of reach. The man kept on talking.

"Makes a lot of sense, really. Not so much work. For some primitive cultures like that, saving their energy was important. They needed to save their energy for fighting the enemy, for building the wigwam, for keeping warm, for traveling their nomadic lifestyle. Depends on where they lived. Around here, I suppose the Indians needed that energy to keep warm in the winter. Winters can get pretty cold and damp. But I guess I don't have to tell you two that." The man laughed.

"Now what tribe are you two fellas?"

Jimmy glanced at Roy. He started to answer, but before he could, the man in the short black coat continued.

"You from around here? I know I've met Indians from other tribes at this dock, too. Maybe just intermarriage. There's a lot of that. But I didn't ask. I'd guess you two are Lummi or Muck-leshoot."

"Lenape."

"What's that?"

"Delaware."

"Delaware. You don't say. Delaware Indians. My gosh. Clear out here on the West Coast." He laughed again. "You Indians sure do get around, I must say. Coast to coast. Well, your tribe fished, too, out along the Atlantic, right there at New York. I've been doing a little studying on the Delaware Indians. I decided it was my duty, living in the United States, to learn a little about all the American tribes, especially if I continue my mission work. So I'm taking a couple of anthropology courses at a community college in the evenings. Now tell me. You know, come to think, maybe I've read that word, that you called yourself. I've never heard it pronounced before now. Tell me again what you called yourselves."

"Lenape."

"Lenape. Good. Good. Lenape. Now that's really something, meeting a couple of Delaware clear out here. Full-bloods, huh?" He didn't wait for an answer, but went on. "You guys are pretty rare. You know that, don't you? You are a rare breed."

"That so," said Roy.

"Why, yes. I just read George Catlin's diaries. Hey, really, I can't believe my luck at running into you two after reading about the Delaware. I mean, Catlin counted only eight hundred Delaware in eighteen thirty-five, and they were in pretty bad shape. Only eight hundred in eighteen thirty-five, and two right here. How about that."

Roy had begun rolling and tying the net and line. Jimmy was gathering the tools, stepping around the man in the short black coat, trying to find the knives and twine in the shadow the man cast through the yellow light.

Jimmy felt tired, a tired he hadn't felt with just Roy. But it was heavy on him now; there was a weight Jimmy felt coming from the words of this man, moving across him like a shadow on the net.

Jimmy's mind drifted away as the man talked on. Like those quiet sounds in the dark beyond the circle of the lamplight, the sounds of the river otters under the docks, the lap of the water on the boats, the call of a single loon, the splash of a grebe fishing by the slender first light of the rising moon, Jimmy's mind moved in the darkness to small sorrows of loss, of the memory of Uncle and Uncle's stories of the place where he now stood. Jimmy felt a sudden cold chill of understanding enter the night like a ghost: the memory of Uncle and Uncle's stories would truly be only that now. Memory. He was gone.

Jimmy could feel the slow rise of his anger as he listened to the drone of this man's voice, a man in a short black coat who would reduce memory and story down to such a low level, to suck life from his ancestors for the momentary entertainment of it.

Then coming again from the dock next to the tug, calling up to the crew on the tug's deck, was Lars's voice. "Fucking Indins. Fucking lazy Indins. If they'd ever work in the daytime they might not have to be diddling with their nets half the night."

The man in the black coat continued talking. "Now one quick story before I leave. I just read this one. Let me tell you quick and then I'll let you go. Though I sure do hope to visit with you again. But the story. You've heard of Manhattan, haven't you?"

"Manhattan," said Roy. "We ever heard of Manhattan, Jimmy?"

"Manhattan," said Jimmy. "Sure does sound familiar. That down by Puyallup?"

Jimmy thought of Grandma One Rock, of what she'd say when Jimmy or Roy or Chuckie would bring home an American history book and be studying something about New York. Ah, Manhattan, she'd say. Sacred place still being used in the same old name way, same old traditions.

Jimmy and Roy and Chuckie knew Grandma One Rock's story. They'd heard of the first ship that had come into the bay and how three men were taken aboard, fed with rich food, given beads and cloth, and served rum that took them on a spirit trip like none of them had ever known before. And in the morning they were left with the first lies, less land, and a new name for that place: Place Where We All Got Drunk.

"Manhattan," the man in the short black coat said. "You know where Manhattan is, don't you?"

As Roy tossed the last of the rope and line up into the boat, he glanced at Jimmy, seeing the anger in Jimmy's face. "Manhattan. Hell, it's all Manhattan to us, isn't it, Jimmy? Matter of fact, I was just thinking about how thirsty I am. What do you say, Jimmy?"

Roy set his shoulder up against Jimmy's shoulder and nodded toward the blinking of the Tides Inn Tavern light and pushed past the man in the short black coat, leaving him alone in the center of the yellow light.

Up on the ramp, the man in the short black coat called out one last time, "Hey, don't get me wrong. I was just trying to help, to give you a little history. So you can begin to help yourselves. That's what I was telling your friend, George, up there, this afternoon. I think education is the key here. Even working on cars requires a certain level of education."

And some deep, ancient, smoldering rage rose up in Jimmy, burning suddenly hot. It was a rage that sent fire through his veins and made him blind and crazy. Consumed by its power, Jimmy broke from Roy. And as Roy tripped and stumbled, Jimmy turned and ran back down the ramp, deaf to Roy's shouts. And as he did, Jimmy knew that it didn't matter now.

Drunk or fighting, it'd be all the same. Somebody would be facedown in the morning, eating dirt.

As he lunged at the man in the short black coat, he saw Lars's face rise from the shadows. Jimmy could feel Lars's blow even before it found him. He tasted the hot blood and felt the splinters of the deck in his scalp and the kick and the spinning, spinning down into the cold water. And he saw his own last thought as if it were written on paper in front of him: I hope they let me work the road crew with Uncle.

Spirit Curse

When Jimmy first came to on his bed in the little cabin, he had no idea what had happened, or how he got home. And the pain was so blindingly strong, it felt like a drug coursing through his veins, carrying him down, down. For several days, he slipped in and out of consciousness. Unreal moments of Mary, Roy, his sons, darkness, light, the sound of waves crashing below the cabin, and horrible deep silence all twirled and spun around him.

The deepest, strongest grip of the pain had passed. The memories, of his rage, of the fight on the dock, of falling into the water, of being pulled out and dragged to the Impala and of being driven home by Roy, were beginning to take shape in his mind, to become a story. And the story became like a bright, hard object in his hands. Something to hold, to look at, to pass around. And finally to laugh at.

Jimmy and his brothers were quick on stories. Sometimes the story would form in their hearts before the experience was even over. They went into their days looking for a story, sniffing it out like bloodhounds. They lived by the story. Telling and listening to stories gave them breath, saved their lives, and connected them deeply to one another. They recognized their kinship by their stories.

But this one, this fight, took a little longer in becoming a story. The physical pain was as bad as any Jimmy had experienced. And the memory of his own rage at such a pitiful man was so strong he could still taste its bitter poison in his mouth.

Finally that became the center of the story, that Jimmy could get so angry at such a little weenie of a guy, a lonely man who didn't know shit but wouldn't shut up. All in full sight of Lars, a fucking Green Beret just back from Vietnam, a hard-drinking, mean tugboat operator who had just been waiting for Jimmy's slightest move to pound the crap out of Jimmy's brown face. And did.

Pretty soon, Jimmy and Mary's bedroom was full of cousins and relations all wanting to see the fresh red scars, hear the story, and bring bits of other stories of the man in the short black coat, of the tug operator, of the docks and other fights. These bits of stories were offerings to tie on Jimmy's pain like tobacco bundles. Jimmy's story grew with his healing until, finally, it had a life of its own and lifted off of Jimmy's chest.

And in all of the telling and talking, Jimmy's story became more than a healing for Jimmy. It became a lifeline for the men on the reservation to hold on to as they saw their own families gripped by a sorrow, a tragedy that no one could ever imagine even whispering as a story. Each telling, each memory, would peel their hearts like a sharp knife, bleeding them again and again.

In the two short months since Uncle had died, four young men had committed suicide: in cars, with whiskey, with guns. Each one struck deep, bringing up old stories of the dead taking young men as companions on their long journey home.

Families were split, torn open, by stories that had become twisted and changed at the missionaries' altars over the years, making Uncle's family feel suddenly defensive that anyone would think that Uncle would steal a son, a child. And with each progressive death, the confusion and fear grew.

Jimmy watched the women cook and talk and try to comfort one another. They rose early and were busy all day and stayed up late in that comforting. Their hearts and their bodies were occupied with the living. And Jimmy watched the men go silent, move from one another, coming together only on days they fished, or around Jimmy's bed to hear some story that didn't cut into the vein of their powerlessness, their sorrow.

But finally, it was Aunt Lucy who called the meeting. She

said she woke from a dream, deep in the middle of the night, remembering the meetings of the women, the aunties and grandmothers of her childhood. And she knew that that was what should be done. It came to her like a vision and a gift, that to stop the death, the women should meet. Whether her vision dream was from memory or from love, it was strong and real and true.

Women from each of the families on the reservation crammed tight into Aunt Lucy's kitchen, around the cookstove, and drank cups of strong, black coffee. The women who did not come were forgiven; some feuds are best left alone for a while. Aunt Lucy understood. Once, an anthropologist had visited the reservation, asking questions about the culture of the people, the religion, the food, the work. He asked Aunt Lucy about the role of women in the Salish culture. She answered, straight-faced and sincerely, To keep the feuds going. Of course, everyone laughed for years at her answer to that anthropologist, but no one disagreed.

But Aunt Lucy knew she had spoken only a piece of the truth, had tricked that anthropologist with just a little bright thread of the whole cloth. She knew it was also the women's job to get together, to talk.

Aunt Lucy understood that things were out of balance, and that to return the balance, the women needed to pay attention to what they loved. There were spirit words for what was going on. There were prayers to call for spirit help, to lift the spirit darkness. There were stories to explain and help.

After a long night of tears, talking, and prayers, Aunt Lucy gave all the women some healing herbs for their families and asked them to keep close to the children, keep everyone in after dark. She said that they would know when the spirit darkness had passed.

Jimmy knew this, and he felt comforted by the protection of these fierce women. And Jimmy was feeling stronger in the day now. He'd chopped some wood and split a few shakes to repair the roof. He had kept close to Mary and the boys since Aunt Lucy had gathered the women together. And twice a day he walked up the path to Aunt Lucy's house, to check on her and Joey, sometimes bringing Joey and two or three other cousins back with him. But when the sun went down, some of Jimmy's pain and broken pride returned, and he'd go to the bedroom alone and escape into the comfort of a dog-eared western paperback.

With some of the money from fishing, Roy had bought the boys a used TV. He hooked it up to an old generator he'd rebuilt. It pleased Mary, because she wanted the boys in at night now, out of the darkness, out of harm until the time had passed. For a couple of hours each night the drone of the generator and the quieter hum of the TV seemed to fill the cabin and the whole dark clearing. But a tree had fallen the night before and crushed the generator. It left the night quiet, returning the small, heartbeat sounds, of Mary, of the boys, of the snap of pitch wood in the cookstove, that Jimmy liked to hear.

"Jimmy," Mary's voice called from the other room. "Jimmy,

I'm going to the store." Jimmy could hear her footsteps come to the door, and the door opened.

"Jimmy, we're out of bread, and I told Cousin George I'd make sandwiches for him to take when he meets Roy and Flo-Low at the dock in the morning. I think Cousin George and Flo-Low live on doughnuts unless Roy cooks for them. And Roy's working so hard, I thought I should send food. But I have to go up to the store to get bread."

"Alone?"

"The boys are on the mattress reading comics. And I don't want them out yet. I will be okay, but I want the boys here. You listen for them, keep them in; I'll just be gone a minute."

"I don't want you out alone."

"But we can't both go."

"I'll go."

"Are you sure? Do you feel good enough?" Mary knew how spooked Jimmy could get alone at night. For Mary, this staying-in time was a reminder of what they needed to care about. It wasn't so much that she was afraid of what was outside in the dark night as it was that what she cared about was inside the house, inside the houses of her relations. But with Jimmy, Mary understood the power of his fear, what he knew, what Grandma One Rock had taught him.

In the first week after the fight, seeing Jimmy so hurt, so strangely broken, Mary was a little afraid for him in a way she couldn't wholly understand. During the time Jimmy had been drinking so hard and finally ended up in jail, there was a stubborn edge to him. It had been easy for Mary to leave him then, to walk away from Jimmy and his path for those months. But maybe there were more years between them now, and she could read his pain better. Or maybe Uncle's death, followed so quickly by these suicides, cast everything in a different light, made this breath, this life, seem much more fragile. Mary felt strangely protective of Jimmy, not unlike she did of her sons, in this staying-in time. She knew it would pass, that Jimmy would be strong again. But she used this time to be careful of Jimmy.

While Jimmy dressed, he could feel his body protest, the pain of his healing wounds rise up, a shiver rise on his skin as he pulled on his cool, rough clothes. He wanted to be in bed, his naked skin next to Mary's soft naked skin, the smell of her in his nostrils as he fell into a dream. But at the same time, Jimmy felt an odd exhilaration at going out in the night, as if getting this loaf of bread were truly an important, difficult task.

Out in the yard at the Impala, Jimmy opened the door, but instead of getting in, he stopped and looked back at the cabin, the warm yellow lights in the windows. He was transported for a moment by the stillness of the night, by the knowledge that that cabin held Mary and his children against the darkness, the wind, and the crash of the waves.

There had been a storm the night before, the sky lit with lightning for hours before the rain and winds started. Then the storm hit the cabin hard, coming across the bay, pelting the roof, the windows, the thin walls. All night the sound of the storm was around them, cracking and felling branches and trees.

Now the yard was littered with cedar and fir branches that, heavy with the summer growth and rain, had been blown far from their trees. Even after the storm quieted, the rain continued hard and steady all day. The air was fragrant with all the smells: the rain, the cedar, the fir, the wet, fallen maple and alder leaves, and the ripe, rotting apples under the ancient tree.

Jimmy knew that with this storm the season had changed. These last few weeks, the early morning fog, the pale yellow in the leaves, the low white sunlight across the water, these had been only gentle reminders of its coming. The storm brought a time of passing and change. Not that there were ever harsh changes in this place. Jimmy understood that. In this place of water and rain and green and gray, the changes were subtle. A matter of shades, of the play of darkness and light, the rising and falling of the sun in the horizon, but always the constancy of water. This place was so unlike Oklahoma. It was a place of two seasons: a slowly unfolding spring that seemed one day to slip into a long, lingering fall.

Standing at the open car door, he saw how small and fragile the cabin looked against all that blackness of the sky, the cedars, the small clearing. And Jimmy understood that maybe that was what Aunt Lucy and the ancestors of this place wanted them to feel from these weeks of staying in, a sense of themselves, small and fragile and together in this dark clearing, a sense that these families belonged in this place.

For many years, Jimmy used to separate his ancestors in Oklahoma from Mary's ancestors here. But as the years passed, he tried and had begun to see them all as his ancestors. Gradually, as he heard the stories, the names of the Old Ones gone before, he began to feel the rhythms and the seasons of this place. And here, when the elders he knew passed on to the other side, he began to understand that those ancestors were his, too, and that finally there was no separation for him between any of his ancestors. This life here, the life beyond, was a dance that joined them all.

Jimmy shivered at the damp cold that had penetrated his clothes while he had been lost in the night and his thoughts. He rubbed his hands along his arms, then slipped into the driver's seat. The Impala started right up. The deep hum of the engine gave him a renewed sense of purpose. Jimmy glanced at the cabin, feeling that same strange tug at his heart he always felt when he passed by on the water, leaving on Uncle's boat.

Driving from the clearing, from the warm familiarity of the cabin, and into the dark overhang of cedar branches along the winding road, even the high beams of the Impala seemed to be sucked up, lost in all that darkness, in the black puddles of the gravel road, the black patches of the moonless night woven in the tall cedars.

It was only under the dim, blinking streetlight before the

big hill that Jimmy sensed something wasn't right, had a strong feeling of a presence near him, behind him, and his eyes caught the white glow in the rearview mirror. Jimmy's blood froze; his breath caught.

Jimmy saw the image in the mirror take shape, the white glowing eyes beneath a black hooded shape, before it faded away. It was there, in his car. Jimmy gripped the wheel and drove up the hill, expecting, knowing, understanding, that he would be next.

Jimmy's mind raced as he watched the dark road fly by and saw the image grow and then fade again, the black hooded figure staring at him with those cold, white marble eyes. He tried to remember. What had Mary told him that Aunt Lucy said to do? Pray. Pray. What prayers?

Jimmy started praying, loudly, "Dear God. Creator. Grandfather. Spare me. Spare me."

Then he thought, panicked, It's a Salish spirit. He tried but could not, in his fear, remember one of Uncle's prayers. He called out random words, hoping to at least get some sympathy from the black hooded figure.

"*Pig^w ad. Syalt. G^wal.* Spirit power ceremony. Cedar root. Capsize."

And then Jimmy remembered and shouted, "But I'm Lenape." Tears were streaming down his face now; thoughts of all ancestors being his ancestors were gone. "I'm Lenape. Oh, God, are you Lenape? Coming to find me here. *Gëtëmak-tunhe. Winëweokàn.* I talk humbly. I am pleading!"

By the time Jimmy said the Lord's Prayer and started his Hail Marys, he was crying, calling out in gulps between the prayers. "I've been good. Oh, I will be good. Don't take me now. Mary. Jesus. God."

But the black hooded shape just came closer, moving toward Jimmy until Jimmy could almost feel it at his neck. There was a red glow now below the white eyes.

Jimmy took the last curve at ninety miles an hour, panting, leaning into the steering wheel. Seeing the lights of the little store ahead, he tried to slow down. But feeling a cold breath on his neck, he steered the Impala straight for the low picket fence around MacDougall's chicken yard next to MacDougall's Store. As he hit, and the sleeping chickens woke midair with feathers, fence, straw, and splintered boards flying everywhere, Jimmy leaped from the Impala, rolling, rolling as he saw the black shape follow out the door and become Aunt Lucy's old black, pointed-eared dog, Bart.

And flat on his back, chickens everywhere, screen doors already slamming, porch lights coming on, Bart licking his bloody face, Jimmy knew the prayers had been answered. The spirit curse was broken. Jimmy knew everyone would be out tomorrow. Because sure as hell, there wasn't a person on the whole reservation that wouldn't come out to see this mess.

Indian Education

Jimmy did such a fine job on the new chicken house that when Flo-Low and Cousin George stopped by to see him in the morning, Cousin George told him he should get paid for it.

"Hell," said George, "before you smashed your Impala into it, it was just an old lean-to, a piece of shit, chicken shit."

"Shit, yeah," said Flo-Low. "If you hadn't run into it, Mac-Dougall would have had to pay somebody to haul away the splinters after the first winter storm."

But Jimmy was just glad that he didn't have to go to jail for busting up the yard, smashing the chicken house, and killing all those chickens. MacDougall had four good chickens left, a whole freezer full of "roadkill," and Jimmy's promise of twenty-five of his best pullets in the spring. Which meant that Jimmy

double-checked each night now to see that their little banty
rooster, Kingfisher, was locked tight in the '52 Chev wagon
with his big barred rock hens, away from coons and fox.

Mary had named the little banty Kingfisher. One morning,
she and Jimmy and their boys were sitting on the porch steps
eating berries and cream and cornbread for breakfast. The boys
had been particularly fascinated by the little banty's acrobatics
in the yard as he leaped and then seemed to dive into the tail
feathers of hen after hen. And so Mary told the boys the story
of little Kingfisher and long-legged Heron. It was a story that
Uncle used to tell her, of that quick little bird's arduous dives
at graceful Heron as she walked in the tide pools alone while
Heron's husband, a slow-moving fisherman, was gone. She
caught Jimmy's eye in a suggestive way when she told the story,
showing him that part of the story, of the irresistible male pow-
ers of that little kingfisher, was meant for him. After that the little banty became Kingfisher.

Each afternoon Jimmy was working on MacDougall's
chicken house and fence, Mary left the younger kids who were
not in school with Aunt Lucy and walked up the beach with
Jimmy's lunch. If it was raining, MacDougall let them sit in the
covered porch. Today Mary brought Jimmy a big lunch and
spread it out on a tarp covered with an old wool blanket, and
they sat in a little patch of the November sunlight in Mac-
Dougall's yard.

"I've been thinking about all those pullets I've got to come
up with for MacDougall in the spring," said Jimmy.

"You sure spend a lot of time worrying about those pullets," said Mary. She unwrapped a thick venison sandwich and handed it to Jimmy.

"I was thinking that maybe I'd have Roy fix up that generator and hook it up to the '52 Chev," said Jimmy.

"For light?"

"No. So we could turn on the radio and play love songs all night for that little banty, to sort of get him in the mood for his mission in the morning."

"Well, as far as I can tell, no male that's ever lived along this stretch of the beach has ever had to be reminded of his mission."

And Mary told Jimmy a story of when she was in seventh grade, after she came to live with Aunt Lucy and Uncle. Her teacher, Miss Morgan, had been doing a week on Indians and had the class memorize Indian colors: red, black, and white. Mary was the only Indian left in her class; her cousins and friends had dropped out already. Miss Morgan had been suggested by the principal to Uncle as a good teacher for Mary, because, as he said, Miss Morgan was good at Indian Education. Uncle came home and said he didn't know how in the hell the principal could know that, since Mary was the first Indian to make it to Miss Morgan's seventh-grade class in that school.

On her week of teaching about Indians, each student had an oral report assignment. Part of Mary's assignment was to ask her family why Indians liked black, red, and white and how they used those colors in their costumes.

That night, while Aunt Lucy was washing the dishes and Mary was drying them, Mary told Aunt Lucy that Miss Morgan said Indians liked the colors black, red, and white. Aunt Lucy paused and looked at Mary. But before she could say anything, Uncle Arnie spoke from where he sat reading a Louis L'Amour at the kitchen table, next to the wood cookstove.

"Indian women like black," he said.

"Why?" asked Mary.

"Doesn't show the grass stains on their backs," said Uncle Arnie.

Aunt Lucy grabbed the dish towel from Mary and ran after Uncle, slapping him with the damp ends of the twirling towel. And they all got to laughing and joking so much that finally Uncle had to give up his book, leave the kitchen, and go chop Aunt Lucy some cedar kindling for the woodstove.

It wasn't until she was ready for bed that night that Mary remembered her report again and went to find Aunt Lucy, where she was knitting socks by the stove in the kitchen. Mary sat in a chair next to her and asked Aunt Lucy to tell her about Indian colors and costumes. Aunt Lucy sat quietly for a minute, still knitting, and then she set her knitting down, looked directly at Mary, and stood up and slowly walked back into her room. Mary could hear Aunt Lucy going through her closet, and she could hear Uncle asking Aunt Lucy what in the hell she thought she was doing making all that noise in the middle of the night. Aunt Lucy just said, Roll over and go back to sleep, old man, and she kept rummaging in the closet.

When Aunt Lucy came back to the kitchen, to where Mary waited for her, she brought three full boxes and set them on the table. And long into the night, Aunt Lucy showed her things from the boxes, telling her stories about each one, about Aunt Lucy's own aunties and grandmothers. Around the kitchen she spread the cedar dress, two small cedar mats, baskets woven with cedar bark and cherry bark and horsetail root and spruce root, earrings of abalone, rattles, necklaces of shell and mountain-sheep bone and bright glass trade beads, and masks and more and more until Mary fell dizzy in all the rich colors and textures and stories.

That night Aunt Lucy had given Mary the small abalone earrings and a necklace of blue Russian trade beads and bone. Over the years, Aunt Lucy gave her other things from those boxes. She heard more stories with each gift. And she watched, too, as young cousins became women and Aunt Lucy gave them gifts from those boxes.

Mary did not get a good grade on her report. On the day of the report, she brought her abalone earrings and held them out so everyone could watch the light from the windows dance across the blues and pinks and yellows of the shell. She passed out the bright trade beads and spread out the cedar dress and small cedar baskets on the front table for the class to see. She held up two masks. One was a large yellow mask with red strips around the eyes. The other was small, black and deep blue.

When Mary was done, but still standing at the front of the room, gathering back the beads, Miss Morgan said to her, and to the whole class, that those things Mary brought were very nice, but she had specifically asked Mary about the Indians' use of the colors black, red, and white, and that Mary must learn to listen better and follow instructions. She was disappointed in Mary. Mary finished gathering up all that she had brought. She quietly sat the rest of the day with her sack tucked away under her desk, and she imagined over and over Miss Morgan's face if she had told the class what Uncle had said about why Indian women wear black.

Later that same year, the class was studying folktales of the world. Miss Morgan assigned them each a country, and each student was to find the folktales of that country and do a report on three of those folktales. Some countries, of course, were richer than others in folktales, and those countries, Ireland, England, Scotland, and Germany, were to be shared by more than one student. Each student, in reading the folktales, was to find the moral of each story and define it carefully.

Mary was assigned American Indian folktales. Miss Morgan told Mary that she would have difficulty finding these folktales, so she gave her two books, one on Cherokee myths and one on Sioux legends. Miss Morgan told her that most of the Indian folktales were lost when the tribes died out in the 1800s. And she explained that these Cherokee and Sioux folktales would be difficult to understand, since the early Indian mind and thought process was so different from that of modern man. But she thought that Mary would have fun learning a little about Indians, since Mary was Indian, too.

Mary took the books home and tried to read them, but the Indians in the pictures all looked like they were wearing yarn wigs, and the teepees looked like they were made of brown cardboard. The stories were all written in nursery-rhyme form. Aunt Lucy got to laughing so hard at the silly books there were tears running down her cheeks.

Finally, wiping her eyes, Aunt Lucy shut the book tight and said, "Now, I will tell you an Indian story. If your teacher wants you to know an Indian story, I will tell you an Indian story. It is a story about Basket Ogress.

"Oh, that Basket Ogress! She was a monster! She was a ferocious being!

"She lived across the bay, up on the side of the highest hill, right up there on the paths to the mountains. That is where she dwelled. In the woods there.

"And the children wanted to go there, to the beach below where Basket Ogress lived. But the parents of the children told them, 'You may not go there. You may not go to her place. She might come upon you folks and she would put you in her huge cedar-root basket.'

"But the children would not listen. In spite of what they had been told, they loaded up their canoes. And they traveled. They went ashore on the other side of the bay.

"They went ashore just as night came. They were hungry. They had traveled a long way. So they cooked some food. They roasted a big salmon.

"After all of the friends ate a piece of salmon, all that was left was the tail of the salmon. They gave the tail of the salmon to Little Hunchback.

"The children said, 'This is yours, Little Hunchback.'

"Oh, Little Hunchback hollered and hollered, 'Oh, you folks! You always give me the fish tail. I want the fish tips!'

"He wanted that good part up on the head, there next to the gills. The good fish tips.

"But the next day, they roasted salmon again. And again, all the friends ate a piece of salmon and all that was left was the tail of the salmon. They gave the tail of the salmon to Little Hunchback. And Little Hunchback hollered and hollered.

" 'Oh, you folks gave me the fish tail again. I want the fish tips! I am going to call Basket Ogress down! I will holler for Basket Ogress!'

"But the children said, 'Be quiet! Be quiet, Little Hunchback. Be quiet. A monster might come after us.'

"But that night, they roasted a salmon again, and after all the friends ate a piece, all that was left was the fish tail. And they gave that fish tail to Little Hunchback.

"This time he started hollering, 'Come down to the shore, Basket Ogress! Come down to the shore, Monster! All I am being given by these folks is the fish tail.'

"The children cried, 'Be quiet! Be quiet, Little Hunchback. Be quiet. A monster might come after us.'

"But Little Hunchback said, 'It's okay if one does come.'

"The children said, 'If it comes here, you will be taken first, Little Hunchback.'

" 'Oh, no,' said Little Hunchback. 'I will always be at the top. Come, Monster! Come down to the shore!'

" 'Don't invite a monster,' the children said. 'One just might come.'

"All at once a noise was heard. It was the cane of that monster. A deer-hoof rattle was tied to her cane. Whesh, whesh, whesh, whesh. A monster was coming now.

" 'No, no! Don't invite it here,' the children hollered at Little Hunchback. 'No, no!'

"But the monster arrived. Basket Ogress was a huge person. She came down, bumping, bumping into everything. She reached the children. Little Hunchback was taken first. He was put inside a clam basket, a big clam basket. That monster carried that clam basket on her back.

"She put another child into the basket. Little Hunchback climbed up on top. She took another and put that child into the basket. And Little Hunchback climbed up on top of the children in that clam basket.

"Little Hunchback saw that the clam basket wasn't an ordinary clam basket. The clam basket was made of snakes. The snakes were woven like cedar roots.

"Basket Ogress put another child into her clam basket. There were eleven children. And each one was a girl. Little Hunchback was the only boy. She picked up each one. She put each child into her clam basket until none were left.

"And each time she put another child into the basket, Little Hunchback climbed up to the top.

"Then Basket Ogress walked back home. She took the children inland. She took them up the trail to her home and she set them down in the basket.

"The monster's youngest granddaughter, Little Up-Rooted Tree, lived with Basket Ogress. Little Up-Rooted Tree had made a big fire. Little Up-Rooted Tree had put a lot of rocks in the pit.

"Basket Ogress enjoyed the thought of the dinner she was about to have of the many children. There were a lot of children! She enjoyed herself. She really enjoyed herself. It was a big fire. She was walking around the fire, teetering toward the fire while she enjoyed herself, thinking about her big dinner of the many children.

"The children watched Basket Ogress go around the fire, enjoying herself, teetering toward the fire. The older children got together in the basket. They said, 'We could burn her up. We could push this no-good so-and-so, because she is teetering toward the fire. We could push her. We could jab her. We can jab and jab her and let her die. We can kill her.'

"Little Hunchback was the first to tumble out of the basket. He was the first one out. He tipped the basket over and all the children, all those girls, tumbled out.

"Basket Ogress was still going around the fire. She was still enjoying herself going around the firepit.

"Then the monster saw them. She saw them all huddled together by the basket, and she said, 'Hey, what's the matter with you folks?'

"The children said, 'We are happy for you! We want you to sing and dance before you roast us!'

"And the monster said, 'Okay.'

"And the children said, 'Step it off, Monster! Step it off!'

"And Basket Ogress started dancing. She started singing.

Put the children by the rocks.
Put the children by the rocks.
Put the children by the rocks.
Put the children by the rocks.

" 'Oh, your singing is really pretty. You sing some more!'

"And she sang some more.

Put the children by the rocks.
Put the children by the rocks.
Put the children by the rocks.
Put the children by the rocks.

"Then the oldest and strongest children started talking among themselves again.

"The Basket Ogress saw them huddled together. 'What are you folks saying?' she asked.

" 'We are happy for you! You sing some more!'

"Basket Ogress started singing and dancing again.

Put the children by the rocks.
Put the children by the rocks.

Put the children by the rocks.

Put the children by the rocks.

"Oh, then the oldest children suddenly shoved the monster into the rocks in the firepit. When the monster fell into the rocks in the firepit, she yelled, 'Take me off the fire, children. Take me off the fire, children. I will return you folks. Take me off the fire, children. I will return you folks.'

"Then the children said to Little Up-Rooted Tree, the youngest granddaughter of Basket Ogress, 'Little Up-Rooted Tree, get us a forked stick! We are trying to get the grandmother of you folks off of the fire. We are trying to get her off of the fire!'

"So Little Up-Rooted Tree went and found a stick. She gave them a good forked stick Basket Ogress used for hunting. The oldest children took that stick. They shoved the monster into the fire. Basket Ogress was neck-jabbed into the fire. There she sizzled on those heated rocks. And she had wanted to eat those children! She would have eaten all the children. But she burned and burned until the fire went out.

"Then the children said to Little Up-Rooted Tree, 'We tried and tried to take the grandmother of you folks out of the fire, but we didn't manage to get her out.'

"All of a sudden Little Hunchback sort of darted off. He went down the trail to the beach. He arrived at the canoe on the shore. He was the first at the shore.

"The other children saw Little Hunchback run down the trail. The children ran after him down to the beach. They ran down to the canoe at the shore. Little Hunchback was going to be in the bow of the canoe.

" 'No! No, Little Hunchback. No! You ride in the middle! You ride in the stern!'

"But no, they did not let Little Hunchback on board.

"Then all the children got in the canoe. They started paddling the canoe across the water. So Little Hunchback threw rocks at them. He hollered, 'That's what you get! That's what you get.'

"Their paddle was broken by the rocks Little Hunchback threw at them. They had to paddle with the broken pieces. It took a long, long time. But the children arrived at where they were from.

"Their folks were there when they came to the shore. 'What did you folks do to him? What did you do to your only man?'

"They were all girls. There were no boys. 'We left,' they said. 'We left him behind. He wouldn't mind. We would stop him, but he wouldn't listen.'

"Their folks said, 'That is okay. It is okay you left him.'

"But then his grandfather went. He went and looked for Little Hunchback. The grandfather of Little Hunchback arrived at the shore. He put Little Hunchback in his canoe. The grandfather of Little Hunchback paddled back to where they were from.

"The grandfather of Little Hunchback asked the children again, 'Why? Why did you folks leave your younger cousin?'

" 'Oh,' the children said. 'Because he invited the monster.

She would have cooked us up. That is why we became angry. And then we just left.'

"Then all the children arrived at the house of their parents.

"That is the end of this story."

And for the next two weeks, after the dishes were done and put away, Uncle had stacked up kindling and firewood for the next day, and the chickens were locked up for the night, Aunt Lucy and Mary sat in the kitchen next to the warm cookstove and Aunt Lucy told stories.

By the end of the week, some of Mary's cousins heard about Aunt Lucy's stories, and the kitchen filled up each night with young listeners. Some were short stories, some were very long stories. There were some Aunt Lucy could remember only in bits and pieces, but as the week went on and her audience grew, more and more of the stories came back to her, stories she had forgotten, and all of them became woven with stories about her own aunties and grandmothers who had first told her the stories.

Some of the stories Mary and her cousins had heard before. They had all been scared with Basket Ogress stories and knew the story of how the grandmother and all her bad little grandchildren who would not help her dig clams on the beach had been changed by the Changer into the big rock with all the little crabs under it.

But there were stories that had not been listened to in many, many years. All of them had to be translated, since none of the cousins spoke or understood the language. More than one time Aunt Lucy had to wipe her eyes in the remembering, in the flood of memory.

On the night before Mary's class report was due, Aunt Lucy sat by the door, knitting, shooing away the cousins, keeping the kitchen quiet, so Mary could write at the kitchen table. Aunt Lucy had made Mary a big pot of marsh tea and a plate of warm ginger cookies. And Mary worked long into the night on the report. She titled it "Aunt Lucy's Indian Stories." For each story, Mary drew a picture, and at the end of the report she wrote a short page about Aunt Lucy and some of the people who first told Aunt Lucy the stories. When Mary read the report out loud to Aunt Lucy, that page, with the names of her relations, pleased Aunt Lucy the most.

Before Mary left for school in the morning, Aunt Lucy told her to tell her teacher that she would come to school and tell some of the stories to Mary's class. Aunt Lucy had never been to school with Mary. She always sent Uncle Arnie to open house alone, making up some excuse or another, some chore that needed doing that only she could do. Aunt Lucy was afraid that at school someone important would discover she could not read.

Aunt Lucy had been so sickly as a child that she'd spent most of her boarding-school days in the infirmary, pressing and mending clothes, until even the pressing and mending became too difficult. Finally the headmaster declared her too sickly and sent her home, where her mother nursed her back to health.

Two years later, when her mother died, she took in laundry and mending to support her brothers and sisters. But she never did learn to read.

At school, when Mary handed her paper to Miss Morgan, she told Miss Morgan that her auntie would come and tell stories. Miss Morgan thanked Mary, but told her that the folktale unit was over, and that they'd be studying ancient Greece now. Mary never said anything to Aunt Lucy about what Miss Morgan said, and Aunt Lucy never asked Mary, but Mary knew she understood.

Mary's grade on the report was the lowest in the class, and as Miss Morgan handed it back to her, she told the class that Mary hadn't included the moral of any of the stories; she hadn't followed the directions of the assignment. And then she asked Mary in front of the class why she hadn't included the morals of the stories. Mary repeated for Miss Morgan what Aunt Lucy told her, that you learn from the stories by just listening. Then Mary said that these stories don't really have morals like some other stories.

"No morals," Miss Morgan gasped. "Really, I think that that is the heart of the problem, Mary. What if everyone interpreted the stories for themselves. Imagine. Why, there'd be utter chaos. To become upstanding citizens, children need stories with strong, clear morals. You must think about that, my dear."

On the last day of school that year, Miss Morgan planned a party and a food drive to feed the hungry people in South America. Each student was to bring two cans of food, preferably meat like Spam or meatballs, because, Miss Morgan explained, people in developing countries never ate enough protein. Miss Morgan told the class that she was proud that her own sister was a dietitian in South America, teaching the people how to eat proper, balanced diets. And all these canned goods would be sent to where her sister worked, and her sister would distribute each can.

When Mary got up on the last day of school, the morning of the food drive, she looked in her auntie's cupboards to find two cans to take to school. On opening the first cupboard, she was startled into remembering that Aunt Lucy canned most all of their food. Staring at the clear blue and brown Mason jars, sitting there like bright jewels on the shelf, she saw canned corn, beans, fish, applesauce, jams, plums, venison, and berries. But she saw nothing that she could take to school, nothing in unbreakable metal cans that could go to South America. She opened the other cupboard to the open sacks of flours and sugars and the cans of commodity Crisco. Her heart sank. She knew she could never bring the cans with the black letters and numbers and the words U.S. COMMODITY FOODS stamped across them. Mary shut the cupboard and went to school, hoping Miss Morgan wouldn't notice if she didn't bring her two cans.

But Miss Morgan did notice, and she had Mary stand up and explain why she was the only child in the class who had not brought canned goods for the poor people in South America. Mary could feel her face grow hot and her throat tighten and the tears come welling up in her eyes. She whispered, "I don't know. I forgot." And with Mary still standing up next to her small wooden desk, Miss Morgan gave the class a lecture on charity, explaining how a civilized world depends on charity. Then she sent Mary to the principal's office for the rest of the day, to think about charity.

That afternoon, Mary walked home alone. When she got to the woods at the end of the long gravel road, she dumped all her school papers in the ditch and ran as fast as she could straight to Uncle's '52 Chev wagon. She got in, turned the key, and started it up. She drove out the long gravel road. She had driven up and down and up and down that road many times with Uncle Arnie beside her, teaching her. But when that '52 Chev wagon hit the asphalt, that was a first for Mary.

And all she knew, as she headed south, was that she was going to California. She was going to find a school in California. She was going to find somewhere where the sun always shone and the teachers were nice.

She had been driving for two hours when the Tacoma Narrows Bridge came into her sight. She knew she was on the right road. She knew California couldn't be far from Tacoma. And she rolled down the window to feel the blast of cold salt air and started singing "Roll on, Columbia" at the top of her lungs.

It was only in the middle of the bridge, seeing the tollbooth straight ahead, that Mary remembered. She didn't have a dime for the toll. Without another thought, Mary spun the car in a wide U-turn. She could feel the fender scrape as the tires climbed the guardrail; she could hear horns honk and brakes squeal.

Back in the yard, Mary parked the car in the dusty spot she had taken it from. Uncle was chopping kindling around at the side of the house. He nodded at Mary as she walked toward the back porch.

"Car work okay for you?" Uncle called out as Mary opened the door.

"Yes," Mary answered and shut the door loudly behind herself.

Mary sat alone in the kitchen that night. Aunt Lucy had left quickly after the dishes were done, not even sweeping the floor. She just said that she needed to get something at Cousin George's.

Uncle Arnie came in with an armful of kindling. He dropped the kindling in the wood box, brushed the splinters off his flannel shirt, and sat down at the table with Mary. It was a warm evening, and the door was open. They sat quietly, listening to the frogs down at the pond filling the air with their love songs. It was many minutes before Uncle Arnie spoke, but when he did, he began to tell her a story.

"When I was a young boy," Uncle began, "the priest came to the village. It was just before the time we all had to leave the village, before the longhouse was burned and we were moved out of our homes. And that priest came to the village, and he baptized everyone there in the little stream next to the village.

"But my grandfather wasn't there that day. I don't know where he was. But that priest had a sharp eye. He saw my grandfather the next day, took him to the stream, baptized him, and gave him a new name. And that priest told my grandfather the rules: Go to Mass on Sunday, confess your sins, don't eat meat on Friday.

"Well, the very next Friday, that priest found my grandfather down on the beach cooking venison in his big old black pot. And the priest asked my grandfather why he wasn't eating fish.

" 'I am,' my grandfather said.

" 'Don't lie,' said the priest.

" 'I am not,' said my grandfather. 'This is a fish. When I killed the deer, I took it down to the river and baptized it and changed its name to Fish.' "

Mary watched her uncle tell the story and laugh, and she laughed with him and felt, as she did, such a deep affection for this old man who had taken her in as his daughter, that she thought she would burst with it.

When they stopped laughing, Uncle got quiet, and then he spoke again to Mary.

"Don't you let somebody else's ideas of this world keep you from seeing and from listening to that good heart of yours." He sat quietly looking at Mary. Then he spoke again. "Sometimes, we must leave to know who we are and where we belong."

Mary watched Uncle as he stood and walked to the open door.

"I've never given you your Indian name," he said, still looking out the door. Then he turned and walked back to Mary and sat back down next to her.

"*x̌atx̌at*. Mallard. The one who leaves but always comes back. That is who you are."

After Mary had finished telling Jimmy these stories, she grew quiet, looking up into the cedars, dark against the pale November sky.

"And that," Mary said, "that is when I knew I would leave that next year, that I'd leave Uncle and Auntie and go to school in Oklahoma. But I knew then, too, that I'd always come back. Again and again."

And that summer when she had left in Grandma One Rock's '47 Nash with Jimmy, heading to Oklahoma and boarding school, the last thing Uncle had said to Mary, before he gently shut her door, was, "*x̌atx̌at.*" And Mary had understood.

Jimmy thought, as he heard these stories, stories that he had heard bits and pieces of before, stories that he had lived in, that he must have been underwater, asleep, to not see it clearly before this, to see who this woman, his wife for all these years, was.

And Jimmy saw now that the trip to Puget Sound, to meet his uncle the year that Mary was only fourteen, was as much just another part of Mary's story, a story already begun and already named by Uncle, as it was a part of his own. And he saw now that his own life was tightly woven, and even named, in Mary's name from Uncle.

Just as he often thought of returning to Rising Sun, Oklahoma, to Grandma One Rock's land and his brothers, Mary's name, her story, was always coming back to this place, to Uncle's place.

And there next to Mary on that blanket, full of her food, her stories, there in the white November light of midday, Jimmy could not take his eyes from her. He saw her eyes, her dark hair, the flush of her face in the cold air, and Jimmy was filled with such a deep pleasure, as deep as any grief or sorrow, a pleasure so very close to pain that it made him ache.

Crashed-Up Cars

The morning was so bitterly cold that just breathing stung Jimmy's nose and lungs. From where Jimmy One Rock stood, out in the yard, he could see the smoke coming from the chimney. The cabin had felt like ice when he woke, but the fire lit easily, and he watched now as the white smoke rose straight up and disappeared into the dark morning sky.

The first blush of sun was just beginning to spread in the east. The very peak of Mount Rainier glowed white like a ghost or a god, far above the bay and the long jagged range of the Cascade Mountains. The stars were still bright, and the sky to the west was so black that Jimmy could just barely see the first outline of the Olympic Mountains. Black against black.

A dream had awakened Jimmy and pulled him out. A powerful dream. It had lifted him out of his bed and Mary's warm, sleepy embrace, the tangle of her hair and legs and her sweet breathing against his skin.

Jimmy didn't much like being up first. He liked lying in bed alone, even a moment or two, missing Mary after she rose, listening for her movements through the small cabin, for her sounds and for a reason to get up. His heart was tied by a string to her, and in the morning he wanted that tug on the string, that little feeling of longing and belonging.

When Jimmy was younger, before he met Mary, before she was in his life and his bed, he liked to get up early, alone. Back in Oklahoma, living in the little cabin with Grandma One Rock and his brothers, sometimes one or the other of them would get up early with him. Usually, though, it would be for some prank, some adventure, some idea they were working on. But on the mornings he was up early alone, it was just to be outside. To watch the night become day, to live in that moment of change. To see nothing in the dark morning, and then to see once again the world, the familiar, illuminated in that bright sunlight.

The first time Jimmy stood on Uncle's beach when the tide was out, he felt that same wonder he felt in the morning. He stood alone, way out on the tide flats, looking at the sand, the seaweed, the shells, the tiny fish and crabs in the little pools, and he imagined it all under water, hours before, hours to come.

That same day, in the evening, at high slack tide, he stood on the logs at the beach with the waves splashing his toes and tried then to imagine standing on that place way out on the sand, now thirteen feet under water. And he was dizzy with the idea. A dizziness he could never entirely shake, even with all his years fishing on Uncle's boat. Not that he would really want to. Sometimes even just looking at the marine charts, seeing those underwater cliffs and mountains, he felt dizzy with the height of it, thinking of being suspended hundreds of feet above land, in a small wooden boat that, at the same moment, felt so solidly held in the water.

The dizzy feeling was close to what Jimmy felt now as the sun rose. It was as if more than one world existed. One of darkness, one of light. A world where the water was there, a world where the water was gone.

And it was that moment of passing, when one world became another, when the world of darkness became the world of light, that Jimmy turned and saw Roy. Roy walked out of the path that twisted through the dark green of frozen blackberry vines and the stark brown of the salmonberry canes, coming from Flo-Low's cabin down the beach where he was staying. Jimmy had come out to wait for Roy, and Roy had come to find Jimmy, both called out by the same dream.

Jimmy and Roy and Chuckie so often shared dreams that it was commonplace to them. Certainly dreams touched their hearts; they followed the dreams and counted on each other as they did. But this was not extraordinary to them, not the stuff of religious miracles they'd heard about from the Catholics, nor was it a joke of cosmic connection.

When they were young, Grandma One Rock would sometimes speak of her dreams, but never before she ate her first bite of breakfast. Any dream, even in a hidden way, could foretell a tragedy, and telling the dream before eating might only set it in motion. It wasn't uncommon for a breakfast conversation to unfold in which they each would fill in bits and pieces of a whole dream, as if it were one fine star quilt, each sewing on his own bright triangles of fabric.

Each would dream, too, his own dreams, important dreams, silly dreams, disturbing dreams, that marked him as separate. And these, too, were often told over breakfast, revealing a little about each dreamer and the worlds of darkness and worlds of light they lived in, the ghosts they danced with.

"Damn," said Roy, close enough now to catch Jimmy's arm with his hand. "I was hoping I wouldn't find you here. I knew I would, but I was hoping anyway."

"Chuckie?" said Jimmy.

"Yeah," said Roy. "You heard anything?"

"Nope. But I thought we could head up the hill to the phone. It's a couple of hours later there, in Oklahoma. Ida Coffeepot should be up by now."

Ida Coffeepot had the only phone for miles. Her cabin was on the red border, she liked to say, where the town of Rising Sun ended and the Indian land began. Not that the town wasn't full of Indians, too. It was. It was just that the stretch of the land east of Rising Sun, that beautiful, poor-soil, eastern Oklahoma land, was still in allotments, held by families whose names and histories and memories told where they came from, why they were there.

And Ida, who prided herself on being a storyteller, a gossip, and a liar, depending on the need, had the only phone on the allotment land. She held it like it was a position, a crown, a throne. Queen Ida.

Ida took messages, she listened in, she gave advice, she tracked people down. She was often left with big phone bills, but the bills always got paid, even if it wasn't by the caller. She lacked for hardly anything, since gifts of food and firewood and blankets and money, like wampum beads generations before, were given to honor her position, her wealth, and her power.

And her car, the vehicle of those messages, pampered by the mechanics, was the best on the rez. It was a two-tone, white top with maroon sides, '58 Buick with deep maroon leather seats. A vehicle that seemed to drive her. When it would pass on one of its missions, anyone who saw it would swear there was no one driving. Maybe it was because Ida Coffeepot was so small. Or maybe because it flew by so fast.

Like Grandma One Rock and her '47 Nash, Ida Coffeepot never had a license to drive that '58 Buick. But unlike Grandma One Rock, Ida Coffeepot drove fast. Ninety was a number she was comfortable with. She flew with those messages. And in all those years she'd been driving, she'd never had a ticket or so much as a scratch on that big, bright Buick. Once she told Grandma One Rock that a little angel sat up on that hood ornament and told her if there was a state patrol car up ahead or any other danger or obstacle to her mission. And she just took that angel's word.

So when Jimmy and Roy got in the Impala, Ida and her two-tone, maroon '58 Buick were on their minds. Unlike Ida's Buick, Jimmy's black '62 Impala had had more than one scratch, most of them in the last six months. The last run-in with MacDougall's chicken house had added more than a few. But it was, indeed, a fine old war canoe now with three heron feathers and a string of abalone buttons hanging from the mirror, a gift from Aunt Lucy after it took her dog, Bart, on such a wild chicken-killing ride.

"Shit, Jimmy," said Roy, rewiring the door shut. "I don't know what trouble Chuckie could have gotten into that could have possibly been worse than what you've done to this car."

Jimmy laughed. "Which makes me wonder what's wrong with Chuckie, how come he's not dreaming about me in this car, calling me to see if I'm all right."

"Maybe Lila's keeping him too busy to dream."

They both laughed, relieved to be able to joke and throw off the heavy mantle of their dreams before they called Ida to hear the truth. They rode in silence along the windy road and up the hill to the phone booth at MacDougall's Store. By the time they pulled in, the heater was glowing red, hot enough to counteract the cold blast of air coming in Roy's wired-open window.

The phone booth was around the side of the old store, under a cedar tree whose branches wrapped it in a full embrace. It was on the side of the store closest to the new chicken house. While Roy lined up a row of coins on the ledge under the pay phone, Jimmy stood under the cedar, leaning against the cracked wired-glass door, both to hear the conversation and with some expectation that there would be some warmth leaking out of the bullet holes in the booth. And from there, Jimmy could admire his own work on the chicken house.

Looking at that chicken house, Jimmy allowed himself to daydream and imagine the chicken house, the fenced-in yard, and the house that he would someday build for Mary and his sons. It would be a strong, beautiful house, facing the water, with French doors and windows that all opened to the salt air in the summer and shut tight in the winter to hold in the warmth from a glowing potbellied stove, singing with the crack of pitchy firewood.

And yet, before that image could fade or alter in his mind, a clear image of a squared-log cabin, freshly chinked, with small paned windows, a stone foundation, a stone chimney, and a covered porch, came up. Jimmy saw the blue cornflowers and a big sycamore, and he knew the cabin was in Oklahoma. Even his daydreams, Jimmy thought, were two-tone, like Ida's big '58 Buick, one color here, one color Oklahoma. Always.

"Oh, the damned line is busy," said Roy. He dropped in one ringing quarter and started dialing again. "I should have guessed. Shit, what Ida needs is a switchboard and a whole row of little operators. Little Choctaw operators all in a row. Now that's a nice image, isn't it, on a goddamned freezing

December morning. Sweet little Choctaw operators, warms me up to just think about what . . ."

But Roy's words were muffled by a little red Thunderbird pulling in next to Jimmy's Impala, up in front of the store. Jimmy watched through the branches of the cedar and saw Dave Patterson and Bill Martin get out of the shiny red, sporty car. They stretched in the December sun like old cats. Each stood by their door and leaned across the hood of the car to face each other.

"Jesus, that's a long drive at this hour for a lousy cup of coffee and a sweet roll," said Dave.

"And look," said Bill, holding up his arm to check his watch. "The place isn't even open yet. Second Saturday we've done that, get here too early."

"I don't know," said Dave. "I'm thinking we might have to pull those little apron strings back in. At least keep 'em tied up until the coffee and sweet rolls are hot on Saturdays."

"Oh, well," said Bill. "Remember the rosemaling period only lasted a couple of months. This antique painting won't go on all that long. I'll bet on it."

"You're probably right," said Dave. "Gives the girls a little fun, and they'll be back. But this Saturday morning class, I don't know. You'd think that somebody would figure that most of those gals have husbands at home on Saturday mornings. Tuesday afternoons would sure make more sense, if you ask me. A day when we're at work, and they've got all that time on their hands. They could use a little something midweek to keep them out of the shopping center, keep those charge cards shut up in their purses."

"Ah, Dave," said Bill. "Maybe we've got it all wrong. Maybe it's just that we're settling for too little on Saturday mornings. Maybe we need our own little hobby, a little something more than MacDougall's hot-crossed buns, if you know what I mean."

Jimmy could hear MacDougall open the back door. Jimmy, in listening to Bill and Dave, hadn't seen MacDougall walk across the frosted backyard. But he could see the footprints now in the crusty white frosted patches on the lawn, patches already shrinking with the first sun slipping through the tree branches. Jimmy knew it would take MacDougall a few minutes to turn on the lights, set up for the day, plug in the coffeepot, and turn on the old furnace that would send out blasts of freezing air as the boiler fired up.

Jimmy once wondered, on the first winter visit from Oklahoma, why MacDougall didn't get one of those timers on his furnace to turn it on in the morning an hour before the store opened. But MacDougall's stubbornness, his rigid daily routine, oddly warmed Jimmy's heart to him. Depending on the cold, the regulars knew to show up an hour or two after the store opened or to dress warmly. But the weekenders liked to point out the cold, in case MacDougall had missed it. And Jimmy had watched MacDougall's face many times, until he imagined he could read MacDougall's mind saying, You're the one who insists on sitting there drinking coffee in the freezing cold, not me. True, MacDougall wasn't always a friendly guy, but you always knew where you stood, that he'd give you as much room to do your own business as he expected you to give him to do his own. And Jimmy had particularly liked that about MacDougall after he smashed up MacDougall's chicken house and had to build a new one for him.

Roy hung up the receiver again, and then immediately picked it up and started putting coins in slots again.

"Maybe everybody else off the rez dreamed about Chuckie last night, too," said Roy.

"Either that," said Jimmy, "or the word's out on those sweet little Choctaw operators of yours, Roy."

While Roy continued to dial, Jimmy's attention was caught again by Dave and Bill.

"Well," said Dave. "You think that MacDougall fellow could get the door open a little early, seeing us out here in the cold."

"But it sure won't be any warmer in there," said Bill. "The old skinflint wouldn't dare spend an extra dime on a pint of oil to warm up the place before he starts taking our money."

"Well, look there. Here he comes," said Dave.

"Careful," said Bill. "Don't get too close to that old beater, you'll get your chinos covered with filth."

"I've seen this piece of junk all around the county. Who's it belong to?" said Dave.

"Oh," said Bill. "That bunch of Indians down in the village. Brought in some new ones this summer. Way they breed down there, you wouldn't think they'd have to import any."

"I wonder if this could be the one that took out old Mac-Dougall's chicken house."

"This is the one," said Bill. "Driving over a hundred, I heard. Drunk as a skunk. A whole carload of them. Still can't understand why MacDougall didn't press charges and throw the bastards in the slammer. Last thing we need in this town is more drunk Indians driving around."

"Well," said Dave, "from the look of this wreck, it won't be going much further. And other than patching up the mess they made of MacDougall's yard, I don't see any of them working long enough to pay for repairs, let alone a new car."

"Oh, hell," said Bill. "Don't be so naive. Those Indians have always got enough illegal dealings going on down there, drugs and whatnot. That and those checks they get every month from the government. They'll always be able to buy booze and keep an old car or two running."

"You're right there," said Dave. "Can't hold a job for a day. But hell, as far as I can see, all these Indians ever do is drive all over China in crashed-up cars."

Jimmy felt Roy's hand on his collar even before he heard the phone-booth door slide open. Roy dropped the phone, which clanked against the glass as it dangled from the cord. With his hands firmly gripping Jimmy's collar, Roy said, "Don't pay them any mind, Jimmy. MacDougall will take care of them in a minute. First he'll pour some of that battery acid he calls coffee down their throats, then he'll freeze their nuts off on those metal swivel stools. Hell, Jimmy, relax. In ten minutes those two will be gutless and nutless." Both Roy and Jimmy laughed. Then Roy let go of Jimmy, reaching for the phone as he said, "Oh, here. It's ringing now."

Jimmy kept his eyes on Roy's face, feeling numb with the cold, with the news he knew Roy was getting. It was always easy to tell how good or bad the news from home was by the gossip and stories Ida gave first. The longer the gossip went on, the easier the caller felt, knowing that bad news always rose quickly in Ida's conversation. The news of Chuckie and Lila came up early, Jimmy could tell.

Roy's head was down, his eyes watching his own feet shuffle the dust and dirt and cigarette butts on the phone-booth floor, one hand on the receiver at his ear, one hand flipping a quarter across his palm.

Roy looked up at Jimmy only long enough to cover the mouthpiece and whisper, "Fire. The old place. And Lila's gone, disappeared."

"Chuckie?" asked Jimmy.

"He's okay."

Jimmy and Roy didn't speak again until they were in the car, icy air blasting out from the cold heater.

"Goddamn, you'd think MacDougall would come out and warm this up for us," said Roy. "All the business we give his phone booth. Least he could do for us." They both laughed.

"Well, tell me. Lila set the fire?" asked Jimmy.

"Either that, or it started somehow at some big party she

had while Chuckie was up at Bartlesville for a few days. Guess Lila had some big thing going there while he was gone. And now Chuckie's kind of taken up where the party left off."

"Drinking?"

"Yeah. Ida went out early this morning, after she got the word from the fire department. She found Chuckie up there, pretty well gone by then. Ida said he had a big old stick and was poking through the ash and embers, blubbering and crying about some canned ham that he thought should be done by now."

Both Roy and Jimmy laughed. They each shook their heads, thinking of their brother.

"Ida washed him down good with a bucket of freezing cold spring water, wrapped him in her big Pendleton traveling blanket, loaded him into her Buick, and drove him to her place. She fed him some stew, and now she has him sleeping in the back room. Deaf Rogers is back with Chuckie now, keeping an eye on him."

"But the old place. It's gone."

"It's gone. The wellhouse is there. And the big sycamore. Lost a couple of branches over the eaves. But it's still there."

Jimmy pulled out his wallet and found the folded, cracked, black-and-white snapshot of Grandma One Rock's old cabin that he always kept with him, a picture Uncle Jake had taken years ago. It had been a perfect spring day. The sycamore was in full leaf, spreading over the covered porch and stone steps.

Jimmy fumbled with it, smoothing it, turning it again and again into the December light, as much as anything to do something to keep from crying.

Choking back the tears, Jimmy said, "Shit, you know, I bet Uncle Jake's still got those logs in his barn. Remember them?"

"I dreamed about them. That's what got me out of bed. That and Grandma One Rock coming to me clear as day, saying, 'There's work to be done.' "

"All I saw was the fire." Jimmy was crying hard now, wiping his eyes with one sleeve, holding the picture out to keep the tears from falling on it.

"Remember how Uncle Jake argued with her about putting those logs away, telling her none of us boys would give a good goddamn about building a log cabin, that we'd hit the road running and the old place would just turn to dust. But Grandma One Rock looked right up at Uncle Jake and said, '_Këlamahpi._' Do as I say. Like she was talking to us boys."

"When do you remember Grandma One Rock ever losing an argument?" Jimmy laughed now, wiping his eyes and remembering the terror that tiny old, old woman could strike in grown men's hearts with just a look.

"December's just as good a time for building a log cabin as any, I'd say. Ida said the stone foundation is still there."

"Hell," said Jimmy. "Chicken house. Log house for Chuckie. All the same. I'm ready."

. . .

Full and warm from a big breakfast with the boys, Jimmy stood and watched the two youngest boys looking at comics, stretched out on the mattress together. And he tried to imagine the older boys on the school bus, as if it were an image he could hold like a snapshot in his heart as he drove the long road to Oklahoma.

Years ago, after a good fishing season, Jimmy and Roy bought tickets and flew back to Oklahoma. But they did that only once. They never did it again, even when their pockets were full of money. Jimmy knew that airplanes played tricks with one's mind and soul, fooling one into believing distances were not so great. He knew he needed to feel every mile, to understand that long lonely distance, to have each turn of the tires pressed into his heart.

Jimmy shut the door quietly behind him and walked across the little porch and down the wooden steps to the Impala, where Roy and Mary were loading the last of Roy and Jimmy's things in the trunk next to the sacks of food for the trip. Though the sun was full and bright now, the wind had picked up off the water and Jimmy hunched his back against its cutting cold.

Jimmy put his arm around Mary's shoulders and felt her move into him. Roy slammed the trunk tight and rubbed his hands together.

"Well, Jimmy Boy. Time to get in that crashed-up car and drive all over China."

"China," said Mary. "I thought you were going to Oklahoma." Mary put her arms around Jimmy.

"Hell," said Jimmy. "You put a couple of Indians in a crashed-up car, you never can tell where they'll end up."

Jimmy kissed Mary. He looked into her eyes, memorizing them for the long trip, for the time he'd be gone, feeling already how the click of the car door as it shut would cut her so far away from him.

And even as the Impala roared up the long drive, bouncing through the potholes into the cover of the ancient cedars, Jimmy thought that if ever his heart should break, it would be someplace in the middle of the long road between this beach and Oklahoma. His heart was always pulled so hard both ways. It was as if he had two rubber bands attached to his heart, one pulled to Mary, one pulled to Oklahoma and to Grandma One Rock's stories and her place on that land. Mary. Grandma One Rock.

Jimmy shook his head and said to Roy, "Women. They sure can get to you, can't they."

"Yeah. I was just thinking of those little Choctaw girls myself, thinking of picking up the phone and hearing the sound of a sweet Choctaw voice in my ear," said Roy. "Think Ida'll go for my idea?"

"What I say, Roy, is that there's no reason not to dream. Hell, as far as I can see, no reason at all."

Where the Road Leads

The evening was clear and cold, the sky a deepening blue. As the Impala turned down Portland's Burnside Street, Jimmy watched the dark shapes of people hunched against the bite of the December wind. And he wondered if anyone on the streets even knew the color of the sky, or cared. For all these people knew in the city, outside was just something to get through to take you to the next building, the next warm box.

Jimmy felt the old thirst coming on him, creeping down his spine, tugging at his every cell. Thirsty for a drink. But he knew it wasn't so much for the drink as it was for the company of drinkers.

Jimmy was surprised at how quickly the panic hit him. He and Roy had just pulled into the city. Hours gone from Mary, days away from Chuckie. Minutes in Portland and already he was needing a drink to fight the loneliness.

"I don't know, Roy," said Jimmy. "Maybe we should just go on, drive a little longer tonight, see how far we can get."

"Hey, it's my cash tonight," said Roy. "A big steak, a soft bed at the Mallory, a TV. We're going to be sleeping in the back of the car soon enough."

Jimmy pulled the car into the Mallory lot, between a new Chrysler and a Volvo. They both laughed when they looked around the lot at the other cars.

"Well, from the looks of this lot, I'd say we missed the pow-wow by a couple of light-years," said Jimmy.

"Hey, careful. We don't want any of that cheap new paint on this war canoe."

"Hell, we'll get out on the open road soon enough and that good dust'll polish the cheap stuff off."

"You check us in, will you? I'll be back in an hour or so. And then we can get those steaks," said Jimmy as he reached over to help Roy wire the door shut again.

"You okay, Jimmy?" Roy looked directly at him. He knew Jimmy was thinking of drinking. But they both knew nothing could be said.

"Yeah. Just need to stretch my legs. Get a little air before I go in. This Indin needs to smell the river to know he's alive," said Jimmy.

"You go ahead and smell the stinking old Willamette," said Roy. "It might save me the price of a steak dinner."

Jimmy lifted his hand in farewell and turned down the side-walk, pulling up his collar close around his neck. He didn't know what he was looking for, but there was something.

There were girls out on the street already. Good-looking girls, short tight skirts, long legs, dark hair and eyes. Indian girls. He knew they were watching him, reminding him that his blood ran hot in his veins.

But he turned down the other side of the street and moved on down the block, hungry for something to make some sense of the odd lonesome feeling that was sweeping over him. He knew he wanted a drink bad, in some dark smoky bar, where the music and the laughter and the sweat and cigarette smoke and soft bodies of strange women could bump up against him, swirl together into one sweet buzz, where mind and body and soul became pure electric energy, white light. And he knew he'd have to walk, walk until he found what he needed to fill that hole in his heart.

In just the short time since he'd pulled up in the Impala with Roy, the city had changed. The buildings had emptied, the stores closed. Lights brightened in the darkening night and shadows grew and took form.

Jimmy felt a tug on his sleeve and turned to see a man who called to him, "Hey, got a quarter for me tonight?"

"Sure," said Jimmy. He reached in his pocket and pulled out all of his loose change, dropping it into the open hand.

"Thank you, my friend. Thank you."

Jimmy extended his hand. "My name's One Rock. Jimmy

One Rock. Lenape from Oklahoma, up by Rising Sun. But I've been up on Puget Sound with my wife's family. You from around here?"

"I'm Frank Stands Alone. Pine Ridge. Sioux."

"Oh, yeah? I met a Stands Alone once. A cousin of my wife's uncle. Came to visit us once, years ago," said Jimmy. He moved into the shadows with Frank, feeling the stories coming on, as if he were falling, slack-kneed, into the arms of something familiar.

"More than one of us Stands Alone. That's for sure. But we're all relations one way or another. I lived up there for a while, up in Washington. A friend of mine was a commercial fisherman. Port Angeles. One night we were working on this boat and up comes this guy and starts in about the fish and how it was my fault and I'm telling him it wasn't my fault, because the only way a salmon ever gets to Pine Ridge is in a can. But he was one of those stone-deaf white guys who just couldn't hear me.

"So pretty soon, I have to grab him and put him up on the hood of this car parked there. And I keep saying to him, 'It's not me, you got it all wrong.'

"But can he hear me? Hell, no. All he can see is my black hair, and I look like the Indian who took his fish. And he says, 'You fucking Indian, two percent of the population and you want fifty percent of the fish. I've got a payment on my boat, why don't you make it for me if you're so goddamned rich.'

And I keep saying, 'It's not me, you got it all wrong.' Well, the guy just wasn't listening to me, so I'm slapping him now. My friends are trying to pull me off, they say, 'Don't, c'mon Frank,' and I say, 'I'm not hurting him, I'm just trying to wake him up.' But I left the next day. I'm Sioux. My heart just wasn't in it. I've got a college degree, but my heart just wasn't in that either."

Frank looked down the street and then back at Jimmy. "I've got another story. Here." He pointed. "Have a seat. Sit down."

Jimmy leaned against the garbage can, listening to the sounds of the city around them, voices from the corner calling out to Frank. A bus passed. A car stopped across the street, the car door opened, there were shouts and curses, and a woman's voice rose high and loud as the car sped away, "Goddamned AC-DC bastard, cucumbers are better than men any day."

Frank lit a cigarette and held out the pack to Jimmy. "No thanks. But thanks."

"So," began Frank, "there are two wagon trains going across the plains. One is a regular train and the other is a circus train. The first one comes to a real bad bump and gets over it and nothing falls out. Then the circus wagon hits the bump and a little baby monkey falls out. The circus wagon doesn't notice the baby monkey has fallen out and it goes on and disappears into the distance." Frank pointed on down the street and both Jimmy and Frank saw in their mind's eye that wagon disappear into the night air, beyond the streetlights and the black crisscross outlines of the bridges over the Willamette.

"Some time goes by," continued Frank, "and a Sioux war party comes riding up." Frank puffed up his chest, pumped his elbows, riding his pony along with the Sioux war party. Frank's teeth were bad, his long hair was tucked into his coat. He wasn't drunk; he didn't smell drunk to Jimmy, just the stale smell of living on the streets.

"The war party finds the baby monkey and takes it back to the village, and they ask one of the elders, 'What is this?' The elder takes that monkey real gently into his arms." Frank cradled his arms, rocking slowly as if he were holding a newborn baby.

"The elder takes the baby monkey into his teepee and tells the people he will think about it. Everyone waits. All the people wait. But you know how they all love to gossip and talk about what's going on. Well, they were about going crazy waiting. Finally, after three days, the elder comes out and stands in front of all the people.

"The people all begin asking him, 'What is it, what is it?' He is quiet for a minute." Frank stood still, hands across his chest. "And then the elder says, 'Well, it has hands just like us and ten fingers. It has a head and a body just like us. It has two legs and feet and ten toes. Just like us. And it's a boy.' "

"But it has hair all over. And it has a long tail. Just like a cow. So the elder says, 'It must be a cowboy.' "

Jimmy and Frank laughed, enjoying the story, the night, that instant feeling of being comrades of the heart in the dark city night. Understanding everything together. Understanding nothing. Knowing that understanding doesn't mean nearly as much as being together, even just a few minutes.

"Thirsty?" Frank asked.

"No," Jimmy lied.

"Hell, me neither," said Frank. "Not yet anyway. Quit drinking for a while. I had a good job. College education. First in my family to get past grade school. But finally, I thought, I'm a Sioux, what's the point. And I fell off the wagon. Except there's no question what I am. Same as you. Just a couple of fucking Indians, huh?

"You know, I asked my grandfather one time why he wasn't bitter. Grandpa said, 'What do you do if a white man wants something you have so bad that he'll kill you? What will make you both happy? Give it to him. Land? Ah, it doesn't matter who has it because nobody really owns land. It's the responsibility of it, that's what.'

"You know, white people are like Ford cars. You run 'em and run 'em and then the alternator gives out, the engine gets balky, and it stops and won't go any further. It can't be renewed. Sioux are the center of the world. We renew ourselves every year at the Sun Dance. We renew. White people don't. That's the difference.

"You know a lot of us are drinking, but we still treat the kids good and the women, and of course the elders. Always the elders. It has to keep going, we have to keep teaching. I used to lecture at colleges. I tried to tell them in those colleges. But I'm Sioux, and finally my heart wasn't in it."

The calls to Frank from the corner got louder; Jimmy could see paper sacks of bottles passed under the streetlight, white puffs of breath rising.

"It's not what's been done to us or to the world," Frank said. "It's how we embrace it. We gotta enjoy this life or else what's left to us is TV."

Jimmy felt the smooth white shell he had been fingering in his pocket and pulled it out into his hand. As he shook hands with Frank, he passed it to him. Jimmy watched Frank turn and walk to his friends on the corner. He stuffed his hands back into his pockets and walked across the dark street.

Jimmy hoped he could find Roy. Because suddenly the thirst and the hunger were unbearable. He felt alone; the world had suddenly fallen away from him, leaving him feeling so heavy, as if his shoes were sunk into the concrete of the street. His eyes searched the night, seeking the lights of the windows of the hotel, wanting to fix his eyes on a light that would pierce the circle of darkness around him.

Acknowledgments

I am grateful to:

Thom Hess, who was there to catch the breath and music of the Lushootseed language and who has continued to share it, again and again.

Vi Hilbert, who encourages us all to tell our stories. Even those Coyote stories.

George Witte, a fine editor, and his able assistant, Josh Kendall. After a couple of missed connections, I am happy and grateful that you found me.

My friends along the way. Keith and Jackie Anna, Larry Ahvakana, Dot and John Fisher-Smith, Joanie Nissenberg, Mary Randlett, George Fence, Nora and Dick Dauenhauer, the Kolb family, Peg Deam, Greg George, Cliff Trafzer, Sherri Schultz, and Paul Kikuchi. And many more. Thank you.